Spectral Tower

By

Remy J. Kirkham

PROLOGUE

STANLEY'S DREAM

In a white dress and blue sweater, Thel stood atop the deck of a lifeguard tower. Her hands gripped the railing as her hair drifted along to the current of a soft wind. Not far from the tower was a garden filled with countless flowers that included the white lotus and Creeping Jenny. Birds sang like tiny flutes from within trees, forever fixed in their attained glory. A river flowed into a lazy pool of water, covered by the glassy reflection of a star-filled night. Grass bubbled up between trees and natural stones alike. And beyond the garden stood a spectacular city, comprised of mountainous buildings all made of crystal. One was so tall it disappeared into the infinity of space. A strawberry-colored mist swirled down between each crystal wall to the cobblestone streets, filled with horse-drawn carriages, bicyclists and pedestrians. Every citizen had a face intoxicated with contentment. Some strolled along with parasols. Others lingered by a huge cornucopia, turgid with fruits and vegetables. All the while a sweet smell drifted through the air…

And this is where it all began to fade. All those images disappeared until there was nothing left. Only Thel remained. And there were these two red teardrops rolling down her face. But she revealed no manner of sadness in the richness of her brown eyes. Rather, she maintained a gaze of tranquility along with a balmy smile. Then she let go of the rail and held her hand up to me. Words drifted from her lips, words so faint yet clear enough to mean so much more than just a dream.

She said…

   "Take my hand before it's too late."

   But this fire erupted out of nowhere. It became a ring, surrounding the tower, surrounding Thel. It rose up around her...

CHAPTER 1

"…Can Wisdom be put in a silver rod?

Or Love in a golden bowl?"

William Blake

(From the Book of Thel)

I threw off the blankets and sat up. But there was no fire. It was just the bleak shadows of my room, humming with silence. And right when I rationalized it to be a bad dream, my eyes were drawn to something strange on the window.

My mouth dropped while my fingers dug deep into the sheets. It looked like stained glass, the kind you'd see in a medieval church. Finally, I slid my way out of bed and cautiously advanced towards the window.

When I stepped closer, my legs almost buckled. For within the framework of the window was a magnificent work of art. It was a lifeguard tower in a Dutch façade. *And there on the top deck stood Thel.*

Her white dress glowed within the darkness of the room. Her face was pallid and translucent, her expression impassive. Her liquid brown eyes glowed from the moon's ghostly rays that penetrated the window. This image both captivated and terrified me. For *this work of art* sprang straight out from the dream I just had.

Thel stood in the tower, a place where we used to sojourn for hours into the night. I could already hear the sound of the waves crashing, resonating like church bells in my head. And her voice…I could still hear it…so clear, so distinct.

Take my hand before it's too late!

Wondering if the dream weren't yet over, I gazed deep into this image of brushstrokes, creating an inexhaustible frontier of precision and delicacy. And I knew right away this had to be Thel's work, marked by her own artistic style. She was a great artist in her own right. So here before my very eyes appeared her own creation. This was her work of art; my dream painted onto a window. But born from whose intelligence? Mine? Hers? Here I stood in a dark room. And there she stood in the tower. The creator became the created, osmosis blurring the distinction between the artist and the dreamer.

Abruptly, a force of anger and horror struck. It came out of nowhere, a violent disturbance finding its way in. Thereupon it built with such rapacious strength. Was it all because of this image on the window? For some reason, it triggered these volatile emotions. And I don't know why.

All I know is that I now wanted to destroy the image of the tower…even of Thel. No longer could I stand the sight of her. How disturbing. Already I cocked my fist and prepared to throw it through the glass.

But I immediately noticed on Thel's right cheek those two red teardrops. I took a breath. And soon the volatility began to fade until it dissolved like a salt doll thrown into a river.

Somehow those red teardrops calmed me as did her watery brown eyes. Like getting lost in a thicket of plum trees, I could forever look into those eyes, filled with the splendor of joy. And when I tried to touch them, the sanguineous sketch faded away into nothingness. The window became nothing more than an abstract sensation. A moment later I staggered back and collapsed onto the bunk. At that point I remembered what the doctor had said concerning my head trauma...

*The inter-convulsion episode detected by the EEG confirms the **memory loss**. And **you also might experience some hallucinations**.*

"Hallucinations," I whispered. And memory loss.
That's true. While gazing at the window, I may have just
seen a memory vanish right before my very eyes.
And what troubled me most of all was not remembering a
thing about Thel until now. No lie. Six months. *Six months*
since my return from overseas. And during all this time not
once did Thel enter my mind. I've all but been catatonic,
living moment by moment, from each day to the next. And
it's not meant to sound at all pretentious. There's no
excuse. I wouldn't even claim to have gone completely mad.

Oftentimes what emerged from my mind were simple
images rippling with sensational comfort. I'd be sitting on
a rock beside a river. Up in the sky, there'd be white
clouds journeying lazily across the sky. Large trees would
move to the subtle rhythm of a cool breeze. There'd be the
long smooth blades of grass beneath my feet. And across the
river would be a number of wild horses running vigorously
throughout the plains of a natural landscape. It was simple
enough, those images. And that's solely what I thought
about for the past six months. I haven't a clue what it all
meant, but I pretty much kept it to myself.

And now this dream, this dream of Thel ramming itself
into my brain, recharged my dull consciousness into acute
wakefulness. My journeys to a land of wonder had thus come

to an end. The cataleptic picture popped like a small bubble drifting through the air. A spell had been broken. And those simple images of a natural landscape weren't so clear anymore. All I could now think about was Thel, the image on the window and why it increased my tension for violence-enough to nearly throw my fist through glass.

And I wondered if it had anything to do with the night I proposed to Thel, which took place at the lifeguard tower…the place where it all went to shit. That's right. For I remembered what she said in response to my proposal.

Marriage means motherhood and death…I'd rather feed a garden and hear the nightingale, than feed a worm and hear it cry…

Even now, after more than a year, mulling over those words caused me to shudder with a faint sense of astonishment. She also revealed a desire to base her life on a poem that characterized life as a wild wisdom, a wisdom unbridled by the tradition of marriage. And I laughed. I regret it now. But at the time, I couldn't help myself. I just found her reasons for not wanting to get married ridiculous. In any case, it led into a terrible fight. She accused me of laughing at her. I tried to tell her that it wasn't her I was laughing at. She didn't believe me. She didn't care. That made me angry. And it all unraveled into a horrible mess. She stayed at the tower while I walked home. And that just happened to be my last memory of Thel. Great. Just great. That was my last memory of her before the amnesia kicked in, when the rest of that crappy night fizzled away into forgetfulness.

So is that why I wanted to throw my fist through the glass? It's quite possible. But there now lingered this distressing realization I couldn't remember a thing about what happened to Thel after I walked home.

What I do remember next is waking up that following morning and no Thel. Granted, there were still aspects of the day not wholly accounted for, much of it still obscured due to the memory loss. For instance, there occurred bits 'n pieces of strange moments incongruent and so very disconcerting. Whether these moments are clues as to what occurred after our fallout is difficult to explain. But what comes to mind is something like…I just don't know…like losing track of time…quiet moments…empty spaces…a void…traveling to another world…And I had a feeling it had to do with my dream or hallucination on the window. Thus the fire from the dream came to mind. But I didn't know what that meant. I only knew these fragmentary images were like jigsaw pieces, a disturbance drifting over me like black smoke.

That one morning I do remember calling out Thel's name and checking every room. I remembered calling her cell phone but no conversation came to mind. I remembered seeing all her clothes still hanging in the closet; all her toiletries still in the bathroom. And I remembered seeing the basement still cluttered with a variety of her art equipment, each instrument methodically displaced from her palette knives to her paintbrushes. The amnesia made it seem as if she never came home that night or that she had simply disappeared. In my absent state of mind none of it made sense. Yet there had to be a logical explanation as to what next occurred after our terrible argument. I'd like to believe she had come home later that night and that we had talked it out. But then what? I mean…*what happened to her?* With all that she left behind…her art equipment and clothes…what the hell happened to her?

And I must've known, for a sequence of events did come together that was accessible enough to form more coherent and crystal clear memories. What can be remembered was how I finished up school with Thel no longer in the picture. I dove into my last semester of studies with a vengeance. Losing myself in school, studying at all hours of the night, I managed to pull off some decent marks in the end. With a Bachelor's degree in World Literature, the plan was to enroll in a grad program. But I got so tired of school. The idea of having to walk into another classroom made me sick to my stomach.

I next recalled this desperate need to get away from *something*. And whatever it was, it drove me to enlist in the marines, to inadvertently follow in my father's footsteps (*a Lt. Colonel killed in action during the Gulf war in '91- sixteen years ago*). Again I really don't know what that *something* was. But it was powerful enough to get me to enlist. If only my enlistment had nothing more to do than being a marine like my father. But no. It seemed to be more connected with that *something*, that *something* central to an inexplicable force of desperation, that *something* beyond my argument with Thel. But I couldn't remember. I simply couldn't remember what that *something* was. Then I recalled the fire in my dream...the fire. But it was only a dream...right?

All that remained certain was the field of action and my own sense of destiny. And sure enough not long after my enlistment, I got shipped off to the Middle East. Though unlike my father, I wasn't killed in action. Instead, I had been severely maimed somewhere in the arid regions of Afghanistan. Unable to remember the heat of battle, I was now being released from the Naval medical center nearly six

11

months after coming home. Administration planned to contact my mother, but I told them not to. We had since been estranged when I told her-by phone-of my enlistment. Boy did she let me have it…crying and carrying on about how all that money my late father left me for school went to waste…asking how I could do such a stupid thing. In response, I just kept apologizing; struggling to explain why I did it. But my explanation didn't make a whole lot of sense, since I really didn't have much of an explanation to give. *All for nothing* is the last thing she said before hanging up. Nonetheless, she did write me a letter while I was in boot camp. And it went straight into my footlocker without being opened. Perhaps I just didn't have the guts to read it. That or I lacked devoting the effort to such moral problems while being thrown into the mud by Drill Instructors; their efforts solely devoted to hammering us privates into becoming trained killers.

Besides all that, my mom had been living in Europe for the past decade. She moved there seven years after my dad's death. While vacationing in Rome, she met a distinguished Italian named Matteo. They fell in love, and she decided to move to Italy for good. Naturally, she planned to take me along, but I didn't want to go. At fifteen years of age I found solace in my mediocre routines with my mediocre friends at my mediocre High school. So arrangements were made for me to stay with family friends. And despite this faint recollection of flying out to visit once, I do know Matteo turned out to be a good man and was also quite wealthy.

In fact, he owned a beach cottage close to where I enrolled at University in 2002. At that time, when they were in California, he had made this bewildering offer to let me stay at his cottage until I graduated. Initially, my mother protested, but he flattered her with endearments that I was like a son to him. I felt weird about that, though my mom seemed pleased. In any case, she expressed concerns about financial compensation. He dismissed her concern asserting not to be troubled with such particulars. Not one to accept handouts, my mother still refused. I did remind her about the survivor benefits my father left for us upon his death; how some of that money could be used for rent. She nearly flipped out and said..."*Absolutely not! That money is strictly for your education and nothing more. End of discussion.*"

That meant I had to get a job. So a number of applications later, I eventually landed one working in the stockroom of a discount department store, a Walmart subsidiary. Never one to see myself as a forklift jockey but what the hell, I now lived by the beach.

Thereafter, my weekly correspondence to Italy relegated to periodic phone calls, sporadic emails and annual birthday cards. Yeah, the part-time job and college did keep me pretty busy. But to be perfectly honest, I was pretty lousy at keeping in touch. It didn't mean anything really. I was just lazy. And Thel took up most of my time too. Come to think of it, I don't think my mom knew anything about her, about how we met and fell in love and about how she moved into Matteo's place only one week after we first met. Previously, she'd been staying in a Hostel after leaving her home state of New York for good. No. My mom didn't really know much about my personal affairs. But I guess that was my fault, being a poor correspondence in the first place. I didn't even bother to tell her my graduation had come and gone…as Thel had already come and *gone*.

Unaware that my graduation had since passed (by a week), my mom did call to let me know she and Matteo planned to make the trip for the ceremony. That's when I told her about my enlistment.

After donating all my belongings along with Thel's to the Salvation Army, I locked up Matteo's cottage for good, mailed him his keys and took the bus down to MCRD (*Marine Corps Recruiting Depot in San Diego*).

I do recall being given the opportunity to study in England after graduation. But I simply found more meaning taking a risk with my own ideals. Jesus! What the hell did that mean anyway? Back from the war, I wondered. I truly wondered, measuring the worth of those ideals amidst my own biological and psychological nonsense.

It took doctors three operations to save my leg and beat an infection. Recovery time lasted up to six months. I still had my leg albeit with a permanent limp.

My physical therapist encouraged daily exercise, that it would stabilize my right knee, lessen the stiffness but not guarantee a full recovery. It didn't matter to me either way. They could've chopped the damn thing off for all I cared. I never expected to survive the war.

Now I found myself at Camp Pendleton, north of San Diego, where I grew up. Admin had recently assigned me to Bravo Company, while I underwent some psychological evaluations. But this therapist seemed way too concerned about what happened in Afghanistan. He wouldn't stop talking about it. He kept asking me about it. But I couldn't remember any of it. In turn he mentioned that I might be suffering from dissociation or hysterical amnesia, as a way of avoiding the war. If I didn't confront those memories at present, he said, they would still find a way to express themselves in flashbacks or hallucinations.

Until now, my only hallucination was of the stained glass image of my dream on the window. Now finding it hard to breath, I considered taking the 20 mg. of Paroxetine. Except what I really needed was fresh air. Furthermore, I wanted to contact Thel to find out how she was and to know what exactly occurred after our fallout that one night.

Though first things first: I had to get the hell out of here. So I reached into my sea bag for a sweatshirt, a pair of jeans and my sneakers. Once dressed, I glanced at the clock: 18:00hrs(6:00pm). That's it? It seemed more like midnight…Maybe it had to do with it being winter. Maybe that's why. Anyway, I continued to dig a little deeper into my sea bag for my field jacket. Instead, what I found was a…*black velvet jewel case?*

I pressed between the grooves and pried the box open like an Oyster shell. A glittering diamond sat within the folds of six small sapphire stones, resembling petals. The ring was structured like a flower, the very ring I hoped to give Thel. And so I carefully placed it back in the case and tossed it onto my bunk. Now I just simply overturned my sea bag to let everything else spill out. Blouses (shirts), trousers and skivvies all piled onto the floor, including my mom's unopened letter. Once my field jacket finally tumbled atop of the heap, I threw it on. And that's when I noticed a string necklace on the floor. It must've also spilled out from my sea bag. Reaching down, I clasped it and saw what appeared to be a small ivory object linked onto the black string. It was an object shaped like a winged horse.

"Pegasus," I whispered, now remembering it to be a gift Thel had given me a couple years ago. She knew all too well how much I liked Mythology, the Greek tragedies and Homer. She loved to hear me tell her all about the myths and what they meant, especially the tragic ones, the ones Thel found so much more interesting and relevant to the human condition.

One of her favorites had been the one of the hunter, Actaeon, who accidentally stumbled upon Artemis-(Goddess of the hunt)-bathing in the nude. To exact her revenge, she turned him into a stag only for his own hounds to chase him down and rip him to pieces.

I could still hear Thel laughing..."Wow! Poor bastard. The Goddess of the hunt, huh? What a bitch!"

But later that night while we were in bed, she said that she couldn't stop thinking about the myth. Something about it troubled her and asked me if there was more to it than just revenge. I told her of one interpretation—

"…how when man finally stumbles upon the true beauty of the world, when such beauty can be so overwhelming, it can at times turn man into a primal beast and ultimately lead him to his own self-destruction, his own primal desires ripping him to pieces…"

Thel had her arms crossed behind her head as she looked intently up at the ceiling. She didn't say anything for a long time. And as I was about to fall asleep, she leaned over, kissed my cheek and said "Thank you." That's it. After that she went to sleep. A few days later she gave me the Pegasus necklace.

Luckily, I had packed it away in my sea bag. Same for the ring. Only now there was no Thel. And that could not last. Refusing to think otherwise, I slipped off my dog tags from around my neck. No sooner had those tags dropped into my jacket pocket that I slipped the necklace around my neck.

Next, I grabbed my wallet, loose change and cigarettes from the night stand and stuffed them into my trouser pockets. Without thinking twice about it, I swiped the jewel case off the bunk and slipped it into my jacket pocket. Lastly, I couldn't forget my cane.

When I shuffled past the duty hut, the Corporal of the guard was sitting at the desk talking on his cell phone. He had a broad smile on his face though gave me a gaze of indifference while prattling away.

And I just kept going, hurriedly stepping away and skipping in leaps and bounds at what seemed like record speed. A throbbing ache ensued where surgeons had removed most of the shrapnel from my leg. Still, my brain buzzed with frightful excitement as I pounded my cane onward. My intent was to go for a short walk, smoke a cigarette and call Thel. But when a white cab drove by, I impulsively flagged it down and climbed right in.

"Where to Mac?" the cabbie asked.
I just told him to find the nearest bar. So as he swiftly motored onto the 5 Freeway southbound, I glanced through the window. The moon had since disappeared. And the sky glowered in ashy gray, as the billowing clouds floated infinitely over the steep and majestic mountaintops. Taking a deep breath, I recollected how I stepped past the threshold as the cold winter lips of night kissed my face. Gradually a foreboding feeling took root. Trying to

overcome another anxiety attack, I fished through my pockets only to realize my meds were still in my room. "Shit."

What my hand found, rather, was the black velvet case. Again I opened it to see the brilliance of the diamond…of the sapphires. It was real. And the longer I gazed into the glittering flower of stones my nerves were steadily restored. The ring brought to mind the old haunts of the past where Thel and I used to hang out, places like Tinker's Tavern and Quinlan's Coffeehouse (*where we first met*). But the best place of all was home, where we cooked together, drank good wine and listened to old Leonard Cohen records. Those were the days of magic, revealing a love grotto…something like the golden age. And of course there was the lifeguard tower too.

My will-to-live now vaporized into a mist of lassitude. I just wanted to fade away. It's true. I really did. That had to be the true reason why I joined the marines in the first place…self-loathing…that vague notion to commit suicide, to die for a cause I didn't know much about. And they sure gave me the chance to. They really did. I swear to god they did. But somehow I managed to survive. And now the only thing I had left turned out to be this fucking ring.

Then I felt this physical shift deep down, lassitude being replaced by fear. My heart felt like a blunt object, bashing my insides to a pulp. I had to call Thel right away! No more waiting. I had to hear her voice and find out what ultimately happened to her. Suddenly a sharp wave of panic struck. I rifled through my pockets for my cell phone. Just great. I forgot that too.

"Goddamn it!" I exclaimed.

The cabbie cleared his throat. "Hey buddy, you alright back there?"

I fell back against the seat. "Yeah… Sorry."
I continued to look at the ring a moment longer…

Much madness is divinest sense...

…a line from a Dickinson poem. And when it came to mind I snapped the velvet case shut. Was it madness? I don't know. The dream? That incredible hallucination on the window? It all made sense to me, in spite of being a little sick in the head. If there's anything that gave me clarity; that made any sense to me at all…it was Thel.

There had to be a pay phone somewhere. No problem. Contacting her was the main thing...The most important thing. Of course I really needed to see her but one step at a time. First and foremost, she had to be willing to answer

21

her phone. She had to be willing to talk to me.

Now there seemed to be this quiet yet forceful motion pushing me onward, the current too strong to be held back. Trying to contain myself, I took a deep breath for it undoubtedly pushed me towards home. I decided to have the cabbie drop me off at Quinlan's. There I'd get some coffee, soak in the surroundings, look for a phone and call Thel. Maybe she'd be willing to meet me there. Who knows? If anything I needed to hear her voice again.

Without so much as a glance through the rear view mirror, the cabbie offered a slow, deliberate nod. I had told him my new destination. Then I sat back, looked ahead and noticed how the headlights split open the impregnable darkness to reveal the highway.

CHAPTER 2

"We're here, Mac!" the cabbie shouted, jolting my dreamless eyes open to a crepuscular night. The cabbie looked fatigued but managed a smile as he held the rear door open.

"Where are we?" I croaked, trying to shake off the last patches of sleep.

He frowned. "I just told you. *We're here…*some coffee shop. Quinlan's, right?"

His words splashed across my face like ice water. Fully awake, I nearly sprang off my seat. *"Really?"*

"Yeah."

He backed away while I anchored my cane and pushed myself up to my feet. Once I paid the fare, he dove into his cab and drove off. My watch showed 18:43(6:43PM) and across the street Quinlan's Coffeehouse bustled heavily with the different shades of faces streaming in and out the front door. I took a deep breath, looked to the sky but not a star in sight. There was only a robust cloud that loomed over like the belly of a falling ghost. And the salty breeze, moist and humid, carried in that intoxicating smell of the sea. Standing in the midst of this small coastal village I heard the sound of conversations come from the patio of the coffeehouse.

After crossing the street, I entered Quinlan's where a syrupy-baked aroma permeated along with the haunting melody of a French song. The tender voice of Edith Piaf crooned *Avant l'heure* harmoniously, blending with the many voices that fluttered throughout the milieu. Nailed to the walls were wooden shelves, filled with new and aging books whilst tables and chairs were filled with new and aging patrons. Some played chess while others typed on laptops. There were a few intently reading books, nibbling on hard rolls and drinking coffee. It's just how I remembered it a while back.

First I went to the bathroom to urinate. Then I went to the sink to wash my hands.

"Jesus," I gasped, hardly recognizing myself in the mirror. My left cheek was scarred, and a few strands of hair had since turned white. I'm sure I was still under thirty. But man did I look beat and just plain fucked up.

Looking into the mirror, I took a deep breath and studied the reflection of my eyes. They looked bigger, tattooed with the certainty my life would be ripped apart by absolute annihilation.

At that moment, memories of the war emerged for the first time. They came in fragments—out of sequence—not making a lot of sense.

Back in the redoubtable smoke of battle, I was somewhere in a small desert village. And thundering flashes repeated at lightning speed. Gripping an M–16 A2 service rifle, I ran past bodies of both friends and enemies alike…headless or disfigured…explosions deafening and constant, the sky blackened by the pouring rain of mortar fire and rocket propelled grenades.

Finally, those images of horror distorted, fading from the mirror leaving only my dismal reflection. All at once a strange, sickening sound came out of my mouth. I fled from the bathroom, stopped at an old wooden table and tried to catch my breath. Hoping that type of fit wouldn't happen again, I plopped into one of the old wooden chairs. It creaked so loudly, I thought it might splinter into a thousand pieces, fibers popping each time I moved. But it held together...so far.

Moments later I noticed a young couple sitting close together on a couch holding hands. They were deeply engaged in a conversation. The girl seemed to be weeping. But then a smile broadened across her face as the boy spoke fervently to her. Abruptly, she threw her arms around him and kissed him on the lips. As far as they were concerned, no one else existed. In their intrinsic moment of love, everyone here (including me) seemed to fade away.

So I closed my eyes momentarily as Piaf's mellifluous voice crooned on. Before long, my nose grasped the overpowering scent of coffee, exuding sweet roasted aromas. And when I opened my eyes, sure enough there on the table was a cup of coffee *plus* a single pastry, submerged in a thick sugary glaze.

I didn't recall any of this here when I sat down. Then again it's possible I stupidly took someone else's table. No matter. It couldn't be helped that the aromas carried me back to the first time I met Thel. She'd been sitting at the next table with a charcoal pencil in hand. Wearing a pair of headphones, she was staring down into her sketchbook. And because her face intrigued me, I couldn't help but stare at her. She had this indefinable expression, a blend between a blank stare and being half asleep, her features between homely and beautiful with eyes almond shaped and watery brown.

And there was her overall appearance to consider. For she simply looked obnoxiously unkempt. Her hair, partially covered by a blue bandanna, fell in greasy strands. A dark green hoodie hung loosely over her body, and she wore baggy camouflage cargo pants, smeared with charcoal stains. As for her hands, I couldn't help but admire the long slenderness of her fingers, showing the characteristics of noble strength and creativity. Last but not least was how she smelled. From her appearance alone, one might've expected an offensive odor to linger sharply in the air. Not so. Rather, she smelled exquisite, giving off a fragrance that captivated me completely. Lavender? I guess it made no difference. For the fragrance possessed such an ethereal power that I slid a little closer to her. Without undo certainty, she caught my interest. But when she caught me staring at her, I grimaced and quickly looked away. I heard her laugh quietly to herself.

My face flushed with embarrassment. Thus I quickly got back to my study notes, sprawled across the table. I had an exam the next day yet found it difficult to focus with her fragrance now sending me into fanciful musings. She fascinated me, and I wanted to talk to her. Therefore I dwelled on a way to start a conversation at the risk of becoming a nuisance.

I reached for my cup of coffee, took a sip and finally settled on giving her a compliment about her perfume. Unfortunately, she had already started sketching. The charcoal pencil took on a life of its own, flying across the paper in all directions. Her strokes were violent, sharp and quick. The lines in her face deepened while her eyes emanated with meditative concentration. I knew right away she couldn't be reached, her face becoming unapproachable. Here was an artist at work, entirely closed off from the temporal world. No longer did a conversation seem possible. And for that reason, I decided to forget about it and get on with studying. A few minutes later, however, the loud ripping of paper startled me out of my own meditative concentration. I turned to see that she was crumpling up the paper into a tight little ball. Clearly frustrated, she flared her nostrils while those long fingers squeezed and twisted that paper with relentless force. My mouth fell open. Conversely, now was my chance to strike up a conversation with her. Then to my great surprise, she flashed me a smile and apologized for the distraction. Utterly taken off guard, I stammered, struggling to regroup my senses. "N-no worries."

She looked away and returned to her drawing, her face drifting off again, closing out the world around her. But I couldn't let this chance slip away…not again.

"I really like your perfume," I said, trying to get her attention with a wave of my hand.

She looked up with narrowed eyes. We had eye contact, even though she seemed to focus on something beyond me. Looking directly into my eyes, she really wasn't looking at me at all. Rather, she seemed to be looking right through me. If ever there was a time I felt insignificant, almost nonexistent, it happened at that very moment. It felt odd, almost terrifying, like being a phantom, invisible in a world tailored only to her existence. But the feeling quickly dissolved when she removed her headphones. Now she was looking at me.

"I'm sorry," she said. "What did you say?"

"I just wanted to tell you that I really like your perfume. Lavender, right?"

She smiled. "Yes."

"I like it," I said, clearing my throat. "Sorry about the disruption…But I just wanted to let you know you smell really good."

She laughed. "Why thank you." And she began to slide

her headphones back on.

Impulsively, I leaned over to shake her hand. "My name's Stanley by the way."

Still holding onto her headphones, she gave my hand a curious glance. There did linger this delay before she released her right hand from her right headphone to shake my hand. It was a firm shake. "I'm Thel."

She quickly let go, while I continued to feel the strength in each of her fingers, rough with calluses. Also, her name took me by surprise. I recognized it instantly. "Thel? As in *The Book of Thel* by William Blake?"

Her face brightened. "You know about that?"

"My Literature Professor turned me on to Blake last semester," I said. "Of all the Romantics, he's my favorite."

She gave me a thumbs up. "Same here. Wow! You're the first person I've met who's familiar with The Book of Thel."

"You were named after it?"

"Yup. Thanks to my father. He was an artist, heavily influenced by Blake's visionary style …" She paused while her eyes dimmed to a glaze, like falling into a daydream. During which time, I noticed how she referred to her father in the past tense. But I guess it meant nothing at all. In time, the silence came to an end when she took a deep breath, rubbed her eyes with thumb and forefinger and slid her headphones down around her neck. "…a great artist indeed."

She quickly closed her sketchbook and held it up. "And as you can see, like father like daughter."

"Mind if I ask what you were working on?"

She groaned, stuffing her sketchbook into this large yellow bag. "Actually I've been wondering the same thing. I guess I just can't concentrate here."

My jaw tightened. "So sorry. I didn't mean to distract you."

Thel looked surprised. "Oh no. You're cool. Like I said before, you're the only person I know with a handle on a Blake masterpiece…" She winked. "And that's fantastic. Besides, it's probably best I stop, a well needed break from this stupid sketch I can't seem to pull together…"

And there was a sudden shift in her tone. It became impassioned. Her eyes once again transformed into that strange hypnotic trance, looking through my head without acknowledging my existence. But I didn't feel nonexistent, not this time. There was something radiant in how she spoke.

"These images keep floating through my head, you know? Rivers…Trees…Grass…Rocks…mountains…brown horses…crystal buildings...stars…terra cotta faces…parasols…a strawberry mist…teardrops…the Creeping Jenny…a graveyard…It's a new kind of city I want to create. It's supposed to be conceptual. The conflict between how man sees himself versus the permanence of nature. But all that comes to mind so far are these weird images, and I don't know how it's all suppose to fit together. Maybe it's not supposed to fit at all. I don't know."

Speechless, I sat there attentively.

She glanced at her watch. "Well…I better skedaddle. It was nice meeting you by the way..." She chuckled. "Sorry if I started rambling. But now you can see why I'm so bloomin frustrated."

When she slung her yellow bag over her shoulder and stood up, I realized I had to see her again.

"Well…Stanley is it?"

I nodded.

32

She smiled. "I'll see you around."

I hastily reached up to tap her arm with the intent of asking if she'd like to meet again soon. But in so doing, my hand accidentally knocked my cup over, spilling coffee all over my notes.

"Shit!" I exclaimed.

"Oh dear," Thel said, her hands flying up to her cheeks. "I'll get you some napkins."

She placed her bag down and hurried off. For the meantime, every leaf of paper was completely drenched, the table submerged in a wet mess. Frustrated, I grabbed all notes wasted and trashed them. An employee soon came to the table with a handful of napkins, a damp towel and a mop.

"I made a helluva mess," I mumbled.

He laughed. "It happens."

I nodded grimly, as he handed me some napkins to dry off my hands. And I wondered where Thel went. Except for her yellow bag, there was no sign of her anywhere. So I just stood there as the employee wiped the table, mopped the floor and took my empty cup.

Eventually I threw a couple pencils and a highlighter into the outside pouch of my backpack, hanging from behind my chair. In due course, Thel returned with a cup of coffee in one hand and a sweet roll in the other. She placed them both on my table.

"Here," she said. "I figured you could use another cup of coffee and something to eat for good measure."

"You didn't have to do that!" I exclaimed, flustered.

She smiled." I know." Next she grabbed her bag, waved goodbye and turned to go. "Toodaloo.

"Hey wait a minute," I called out.

She stopped.

I took a deep breath. "Maybe we can meet again sometime?"

Thel gave me a wink and was out the door a second later.

I blinked, scratching my head with perplexed embarrassment. Now I gazed at the steam slowly rising up from the rich black coffee, and the butter melting over the pastry. With a heavy sigh I sat down, reached for the cup and took a sip. It was piping hot but good and strong.

Right then I noticed a tiny slip of paper on the coffee dish. It was folded in half. I quickly placed the coffee down and unfolded the slip of paper. It said...

Why a Tongue impress'd with honey from every wind?

1-760-5_-8___

I sat there in senseless amazement. The line came from *"The Book of Thel"* all right. But my eyes remained firmly on the phone number...*It had to be her phone number*!

I couldn't stop staring at it. Wow. Never did the world look so good as it did right now. And never did that sweet roll look as delicious as it did right now. Without further ado, I swiped the pastry off the plate and let my teeth sink into warm, buttery sweetness. In a matter of seconds I finished the pastry, washing it down with more coffee. After that I closed my eyes and thought about the way Thel smelled and wondered what kind of body hid beneath all that billowing clothing. I thought about our conversation and her watery brown eyes. Lastly, I thought about when to call her. Wow. What a strange feeling. I couldn't stop smiling. But when I opened my eyes something terribly strange had happened. *And it was drastic!* Everything looked so different. The people looked so different. The place looked so different. It smelled so different. It even sounded different. And the music? There was something oddly familiar about it. Eventually I remembered. Edith Piaf! That's right…*Avant l'heure.* Now she sang a different song, which I didn't recognize at all. In any case, her refulgent voice brought me back to the vast coldness of the present, to the slight throbbing in my left leg, to the sight of my cane lying across the table, where a sweet roll and cup of coffee had once been. This wasn't fun at all. Moreover, there was no tiny slip of paper either.

Thel had also once been here, sitting right across from me. Now there was nothing. No pastry. No piping hot coffee. No poetry. No Thel. No eyes of mystery…not a goddamn thing...not even a shadow. Even so, I sighed with great relief to at least remember the first conversation I ever had with her. And the dream of her in the tower came to mind. Oddly, I felt there being this distinct correlation between the dream and our first conversation. But I couldn't quite make out the connection…

Right at that moment, the white flash of something caught the corner of my eye. When I turned, a chill rippled up the back of my neck upon capturing an impossible spectacle in full view.

...the brilliance of a blue sweater and white dress...

"Holy fuck!"

It was her. It was Thel, the one from my dream, from the hallucination on the window and from the past. But now she looked more real than ever. This time I could really see her, how her dark brown hair flowed down in thick wavy strands, her skin exuding a deep lustrous hue of gold, her blue sweater glistening like the surface of the ocean and her white dress glowing like a full moon.

She walked towards the front door and paused. She looked at me with a smile before she waved and stepped out.

"Thel!" I shouted, springing up after her.

"EXCUSE ME, SIR?" a voice called out from behind me. I turned to see the barista run up with my cane. "You forgot this."

"Thanks!" I said before asking if she saw a girl in a blue sweater and white dress run out the front door.

She slowly shook her head. "Sorry."

A bit of embarrassed laughter tumbled from my mouth. I guess it made no difference. But once I got outside, Thel was nowhere to be seen.

From the patio, the sweet heady scent of cloves and cigarettes wafted up my nostrils. Two boys, about seven or eight, stormed out of the coffeehouse wearing these large purple ties. Holding tightly to their disposable coffee cups, they ran to the curb waving to the passing traffic. And when it fizzled to an empty street, they ran out dancing wildly. Soon after, their mother ran out screaming at them to get back on the sidewalk.

The whole time, a loud excitable conversation took place between a girl and her cell phone. Alone at her table, she seemed to suffer from an uncontrollable fit of laughter while repeating..."I am so fucked up!" And she continued to laugh shrilly, while the roaring sounds of diesel engines could be heard from the distance. As these daunting echoes of machinery increased in their thundering approach, images of military trucks flashed through my mind.

The boys in their obscenely large ties laughed and jumped up and down. "Here they come! Here they come!"

"...-so fucked up! Hahaha!"

"Get over here!" Their mother wailed, running after them. The two boys quickly jumped back onto the sidewalk and started waving to the trucks. A few drivers waved back to the boys jumping up and down hysterically.

"The circus is here, the circus is here!" they screamed.

There was a caravan of approximately six trucks, all painted in swirling multiple colors with tigers leaping through rings of fire, elephants standing on two hind legs, jugglers tossing torches, acrobats swinging through the air and clowns with bloody red grins. Chimpanzees were dressed in black tuxedos and a lion posed in a crouched position ready to pounce. Its mane, in bright golden colors, framed a hard predacious face. The eyes were narrow and penetrating. Such an image was lurid indeed as if this creature purposely elicited a fear, daring anyone to come see such a ferocious act…those eyes staring with deadly intent… "I see monsters! Hahaha!"

"The circus is here! The circus is here!" the two boys chanted, waving and running along with the trucks. The mother quickly ran after her boys shaking her fist in the air. She seemed to float right up into the air…*up, up and away*, as those sounds of diesel engines continued to echo through my head. And that's when I saw Thel drift across the street into the Qk-Stop convenient store.

"I see ghosts! Hahaha!

CHAPTER 3

No sign of her...Only some cashier with a lengthy goatee and dull expression. Far beyond his left shoulder a cop, carrying two foil-wrapped hot dogs, sauntered to the condiment bar. I attributed his bulky physique to a bulletproof vest beneath his shirt. His rimless spectacles made him look more like a lawyer than a cop. And crackling transmission erupted from his radio intermittently.

I clenched my jaw unsure why the transmission brought to mind the ghostly face of a dead soldier. Trying to escape the grip of this unexpected nightmare, I turned down the first aisle looking for Thel. Here on both sides was an assortment of candy stacked from top to bottom. And when I saw the *Da Vida* Chocolate, I came to a complete standstill. No longer was I gripped by that nightmare.

There had been a time when Thel stood here gazing at all this candy, piled up to the top shelf. I remembered how her eyes brightened as she reached for a *Da Vida* chocolate bar, her favorite kind. And when she turned to me, her indulgence changed, defined by a mischievous smile. Without warning, she tossed the candy to me, and I caught it before it hit the floor. Soon we were face to face in the middle of the aisle. Gazing into my eyes, she took hold of my face and kissed me. When her tongue slid into my mouth her eyes rolled back. And my arms firmly embraced her waist. We were out of control. I then rubbed up against her thigh and was about to reach up under her dress, her hand already reaching down between my legs.

Right then, I heard a voice slice through my ears like a knife. "Hey man! You all right?"

I grappled with my cane in order to keep from spilling to the floor. After regaining my footing, I turned around and saw that cashier give me a blank stare.

"You alright?" he cawed.

Forcing a smile, I nodded.

He pointed towards my hand. "You gonna buy that?"

Not knowing what he meant, I looked down and stared dumbly at the *Da Vida* chocolate in my hand. With trepidation, I failed to remember grabbing it from the shelf. A memory playing itself out. Damn. An adumbrative moment indeed. But not that kiss…

"Hey," the cashier repeated. "I asked you a question. Are you gonna buy that or what?"

I staggered towards the counter and placed the

41

chocolate on the counter.

"Is that it?"

"Yeah."

He rang it up.

"I'll be alright," I whispered.

The cashier shot me a look. "Eh?"

"Nothing."

"A dollar fifty."

No doubt the situation remained dismal and pathetic. There was a reason why I stepped into this very store. But to somehow regain a sense of reason seemed hopeless. There was only one way to know for sure. I leaned towards the cashier in a desperate attempt to overcome the unthinkable. "Did you by chance see a girl in a white dress and blue sweater walk in here?"

"No," he said curtly. "A dollar fifty please."

I placed the money on the counter and again heard static transmission. And again what emerged in my mind was that ghostly face…

skin without color…pale lips…marble eyes…

That cop approached the counter. My cane slid through my hand until it rapped the floor. When his radio blared once more, I grabbed the *Da Vida* chocolate before rushing for the exit.

Once I threw the door open, it rattled with a sharp thump followed by a heavy thud. "Ah!"

A giant man with tired looking eyes and a mustache rubbed his forehead.

Shit. I threw the door right into his face.

"Uita-te unde dracu 'te duci!" he exclaimed.

I apologized.

A young woman stepped out from a beaten white Toyota pickup and ran to him. She had black hair that matched her black lipstick along with black nail polish. And she was much shorter than the giant. She gave me this strange look. And when she smiled, a weird feeling overcame me. The hairs rose from behind my neck.

I was about to ask if we had ever met before when the man pointed to my face. "Acest tip aruncat dreptul uşii în mine!"

"Am văzut." she said, clasping his arm. "Te simti

bine?"

"Nu prea," he mumbled, flashing me a look of irritation.

Then she whispered something into his ear.

He shook his head, glancing at my cane. "Da, ştiu, ştiu."

She continued to whisper until his expression softened. "Bine, bine. Să mergem."

Their dialect sounded Romainian or maybe Greek. I don't know. It was hard to tell. Whatever the case, the giant nodded, grabbed the girl's hand, and they strode into the store without saying another word. The weird feeling now turned to hatred. It's true. For some inexplicable reason, I hated them. It made no sense. Why should they mean a goddamn thing to me anyway? It was hysterical. And I felt bad about it. They were clearly from another country, from a different culture. Quite possibly the circus? They spoke a different language. Hell. Why should I care? Forget it. I had to call Thel.

Turning to go, I noticed a police car…that cop's police car parked in front of the store. A little girl, about nine or ten, sat in the passenger seat. She leered at me while on her cell phone, her mouth twisting and turning at rapid speed.

I waved her off, then turned and stepped away to find a pay phone. And I hoped to hell Thel would answer. For now, these hallucinations were getting to me. Seeing her in my room, seeing her leave the coffeehouse and *drift* into the QK-Stop were all but busting me wide open. But again this was the longest I'd been without my meds. And yet those words...*Take my hand before it's too late*...That's what bothered me most of all.

It had to be part of this post-traumatic stress, right? It had to be. But the only way to know for sure was to call Thel. I didn't even have to see her. To hear her voice, to know she was all right would be enough. Find a pay phone and call her. She had to answer. Then I'd know. And all would be well.

Walking past the Toyota, I noticed its Nebraska license plate. Those foreigners were from the cornhusker state? Interesting. But all the more interesting was seeing the passenger door left *wide open*! Apparently bamboozled by my embarrassing run-in with her partner, the girl forgot to close the door. And upon seeing an unopened beer can stashed between the two front seats, I crawled right in and took it. Before crawling out, I also saw this thick book

45

on the dashboard. After slipping the beer into my jacket pocket, I grabbed the book with a title too difficult to pronounce.

Below the title was this sketch of a man and woman kneeling on either side of this small furnace, made of bricks. The man seemed to be praying while the woman poured something into the furnace. She poured it from a small glass bottle.

I immediately tossed the book back onto the dashboard and glanced through the rear window. There were two cardboard boxes in the bed of the truck. The smaller one was weathered and beaten. Bits of blue canvas sprang out from the numerous rips in the box. There was a picture of a blue tent on one side with the specs written below it: 18′ x 10′ 3-Room sports tent. The other box was much larger, in much better shape and sealed shut. No labels identified its contents whatsoever.

"*Hey*!" somebody yelled.

Startled, I backed out of the truck and almost buckled over. I caught my balance just in time. All at once, I noticed that police officer standing there holding his two hot dogs and large soda cup. Just the same, he managed to twist his face into an imperative mask of lawful order. *"Step away from the vehicle!"*

Those foreigners stood right beside him and seemed put at ease-with a vast understanding in their eyes-this cop would take care of business.

All the while, the officer continued to stare me down until the passenger door to the patrol car opened. That little girl had since squirmed her way out and ran to him.

"Oh no you don't!" the cop exclaimed. "Get back in the car, Sara."

She flinched. "But dad…"

"Now!"

And that's when I made a run for it.

"Hey! Stop right there!"

"Sorry!" I croaked, my throat tightening to the degree of near suffocation. A cacophony of screams erupted, mixed with incendiary explosions, echoing throughout my head. And something-like a Will o' the Wisp-flitted up into the air…a human figure. Oh Christ. Not again. It was Thel in her white dress and blue sweater. "I'm hallucinating!" I gasped, chasing her anyway. My face burned with fever. And

I seemed to be gaining on her with each leap and wriggle. But she then drifted through the front door, under the white flashing marquee of a familiar landmark: *Tinker's Tavern*. I glanced over my shoulder but no sign of flashing police lights. I soon reached the spot where Thel had just been. Before going inside, I stooped over and choked for air. My chest burned for oxygen. And as the panic began to subside, I pictured fading shadows revealing a dreary image of half a town in rubble, the other half slipping into darkness. It was like being a part of some forgotten dream that possessed more than one nightmare fighting to be remembered. Sweat rolled down my face as something sickly began to manifest from within. I held fast to my cane and wiped the sweat from my brow. And somewhere along the way, I lost the *Da Vida* chocolate bar.

CHAPTER 4

Ok. So once again I got suckered into believing Thel might be here, seeing how *she drifted through a closed door.* And there she'd be waiting for me at the bar or at an empty table. And I'll be damned if I didn't look around, held fast by the hub of the absurd. Strange compulsions for what's to be discovered; a place of impassive faces, half filled tumblers, a televised football game and two sizable men playing pool. But no Thel. All I saw with a flush of hope was a payphone in the back corner of the tavern.

I pressed on trying to think of what to say if Thel answered the phone. After tossing in enough change to make the call, I felt my heart thump wildly.

With quick shallow breaths, I licked my lips and waited until either she or her voicemail picked up. But after the third ring neither one did. Instead I got that intercept message with the...beep...beep...beep!

"We're sorry; you have reached a number that has been disconnected or is no longer in service. If you feel you have reached this recording in error, please check the number and try your call again."

"Shit," I muttered, slamming the receiver down and waiting for my change to return. Maybe I dialed it wrong. This time I pressed each digit slowly and carefully, confident I had her number correctly committed to memory. But again I got... beep...beep...beep! *"We're sorry;..."*

I decided to call the operator and asked him to look up a listing for a Thel.

"Last name?" He asked.

"No last name. Just Thel."

"Oh."

It's true. One time when she wrote me a check for expenses, I thought she forgot to write her last name on it.

"No," she said. "My father had legally christened me with just Thel. I told you he was big into Blake."

She pointed to the letterhead of her check and laughed. "See?" Sure enough, it showed only Thel.

And I also remembered seeing-on a rare occasion-that her driver's license included "NoName" in the first box. It read...*NoName Thel.*

Unfortunately, the operator found no such listing in California or New York or anywhere else in this godforsaken country. He found no one with only that name.

"Are you sure?"

"Sorry sir. With the exception of a software company, that name just doesn't come up." I hung up and took a few deep breaths. Yeah okay the war drove me a little crazy. But come on! With the exception of the amnesia, my memories of her were simply too damned vivid. And I had the engagement ring.

Where the hell was she? Maybe I took for granted she'd always be a phone call away. But at the moment I had no idea what to do next. I couldn't think of who else to call. I didn't know (or couldn't remember) any of her friends. And both her parents were out of commission: Her father was dead, her mother's location unknown.

"Now what," I whispered, feeling frustrated and defeated by the world.

Out of options, I decided to follow my shadow to the last available barstool at the far end. I needed a drink.

"What'll it be?" Tinker asked, his youthful smile

penetrating through deep wrinkles. I remembered him from my college days. With his long white hair pulled back in a short ponytail and full white beard, he still looked the same. But I don't think he remembered me. His face never flashed with recognition and that's okay, for I wanted to drink without the strained palaver of days gone by.

"Scotch," I replied.

He gave a thumbs-up and walked away saying nothing more. Before long, I took a deep breath feeling the safety of a hideaway from the outward peril of possibly being arrested. Whereupon, I gazed mindlessly at the football game on TV until my drink came. I lifted it and noticed how the glass trembled between my thumb and forefinger. "Calm the fuck down," I murmured and drank it all in one swallow.

That fuzzy feeling quickly took effect once the scotch slid down my gullet. My heart then slowed to a calm, stable beat amidst the stagnant air and alcoholic fumes. I placed the empty glass down.

When that emollient buzz anchored in, my eyes and ears were drawn with subtle curiosity towards the riotous din of that pool game. The two players were laughing and belching away. One had a bloated gut. The other was lean and muscular. But they both had scraggly beards. The lean guy had long black hair tied back into a braid. The fat one had greasy blonde hair hanging loosely in strings to his shoulders. Tattoos covered their arms. And the guy with the braid had one on his neck. It looked like a four leaf clover but I couldn't tell for sure from where I sat.

They moved about the table frequently, engaged in the hard banging of stripes and solids. They talked loud and swore at bad shots. And when I noticed two half-filled beer glasses at their table, I decided to get a beer too.

After Tinker took my request, I noticed this lanky old man sitting to my left. He wore a green sports-cap with a small emblem of a leaping animal resembling an antelope. With white side-burns and a bushy mustache, he appeared haggard, with sunken eyes and skeletal features. It seemed as though the blood had stopped pumping to his head or the world at last had sucked him dry.

He swayed a bit on his stool while staring at a Polaroid in his right hand. It was of a lion sitting on a pedestal in a large cage.

"Beautiful isn't he?" the old man slurred in some kind of accent…British? Dutch? Australian? Hard to tell. Tinker finally brought my beer. I grabbed it and answered the old man with a strained smile.

CHAPTER 5

Finishing up my beer, I raised my glass for another. Tinker gave a nod while ringing up a tab. In the meantime, I saw through a mirror opposite to where I sat the reflection of the old man. With a morose expression, he just kept staring at the Polaroid and seemed to be crying. I turned directly towards him. Sure enough there were tears in his eyes.

"You okay?"

His face flashed with surprise. He then wiped away his tears and placed the Polaroid in front of me. When he spoke, his voice resonated with an accent still difficult to recognize. "His name's Samson as in Delilah's Samson. I named him that from the bible you know…the story of when Delilah seduced Samson and later cut his hair, diminishing all his God-given strength." He pointed out the lion's yellow tresses.

"Are you with the circus?" I asked.

He wiped a layer of sweat from his face, pallid in complexion, almost sickly and covered his mouth to stifle a string of congested coughs. Once they subsided, he took a drink and gave me a sorrowful look.

"You wanna see something interesting?"

I shrugged. "Sure."

He pulled down his collar to reveal a bandage wrapped half way around his neck. The uncovered portion showed a yellow and dark purplish color, the skin clearly bruised and swollen, possibly infected.

"That my friend is a lion scratch."

My mouth dropped. "Really?"

"It happened a couple days ago. Samson was shot with a shit load of tranquilizers before he got the best of me."

His pale blue eyes gleamed as he licked his upper lip. "But to answer your question…Yes, I am or was the lion trainer for the circus." He now leaned closer and looked directly at me.

"Forgive me. But there's something about your eyes I find interesting. That look you have carries a certain sadness, something I haven't seen since the war…" He trailed off, his eyes oozing with their own stately affair of sadness.

I looked away, wishing to have kept my mouth shut from the start. My second beer finally made it in front of me. I

55

drank.

"I'm sorry," the trainer said. "Don't be offended. Your expression brings to mind a time when I was still back in South Africa. It was when we were protecting our borders from those damn commies. Ah, what a bloody mess you know. We fought for nothing and our country went to shit. That's how I saw it anyway. So after that I went into the bush, into a private game reserve, back to the simplicity of nature, where I learned to live again. There I found solace caring for the Springbok, Impalas and Zebras. Life was good until…"

The old man grimaced, took another drink and stared at the television. He looked troubled, and no longer did I wonder about his accent.

"Your break!" a voice boomed from the pool table. The muscular guy leaned in and viciously hammered away the Q ball with a swift stroke. He sent it across the felt at lightning speed and diffused the balls with a sharp explosive crack. Solids and stripes went flying in all directions, a handful dropping into side and corner pockets. But when the Eight ball dropped into the left corner pocket, the guy who made the break threw his stick across the table. "Goddamn it!" he bellowed.

"One time a lion escaped from the reserve," the old man continued. "But we tracked him down by the end of the day. To see him in his own domain struck me with a kind of divine enlightenment. He looked beautiful and ferocious at the same time, lying in the grass in perfect control of his surroundings, camouflaged within the bush. To spot this majestic animal you must look for his shape, not so much his color, or you'll never see him. But when you finally do…" Rolling his eyes, he whistled with wonder.

"To see his spirit glow, you can truly understand the true majestic beauty of this beast. But make no mistake; beneath his majesty is pure terror. Whenever you come face to face with a lion…*stand still*! He might not attack. One time a photographer, from *National Geographic,* profiled a pride of females. And they're far more aggressive than the males. Anyway, he had his camera you know. And one of them sprang out and rushed him. Well, this guy had balls. He wrestled every impulse to run and just stood there. And you won't believe it! This goddamn beast got so confused she slid to a halt with perked ears. Picture it: A guy standing there, still as a statue, sweat pouring down his face while nature's fucking nightmare calmly starts licking his leg…"

The old man rolled back his head and erupted with laughter. "Sorry. I just think that's so goddamn funny."

And he kept laughing until succumbing to a rapid string of coughs. Eventually, he managed to catch his breath and wiped a tear from his cheek.

"As for *our* lion that escaped, we managed to tag him and truck him back to the reserve."

The trainer then expelled a weighty sigh, slumped back into his stool and drooped his head down to his chest. "It wasn't until later that night we learned he had already killed one of our workers. The poor bastard. His head had been ripped off, *completely severed from his neck*!"

"Jesus!" I gasped.

"Now he had to be destroyed. Understand? Once an animal like that tastes human flesh that's it! It becomes a man-eater."

"I've heard about that. But why?"

"Because we're so much easier to eat! Compared to the rough leathery hide of say a Zebra, our flesh is much softer and supple without all that roughness and hair to tear through."

"So you had to kill him?"

"I volunteered to do it. I practically raised him

after all. I just couldn't allow anyone else to do it. I had to-…" He bit down on his bottom lip and took a drink. "Ah hell! Some things you just try to forget! I mean really try to forget…always the most staggering things…those things that burrow deep in the belly and stay in you like some blood sucking parasite."

He gazed pensively at Sampson's picture. "And so after that what did I decide to do?" He lifted his glass in salutations. "I joined a fucking circus!"

He took a drink, cleared his throat and wiped his eyes. "It's sure funny how life can turn you for a loop, like a full circle, going round and round…over and over again, the past repeating itself…sometimes tragic…sometimes not. But it's all repetitive.

'Take the unfortunate Samson for example. These cats aren't just ferocious beasts. No! They have real personalities! Some are humorous. Others are affectionate. And Samson may have had a temper, but he was the best! He was the smartest of them all. And just so you know, I'm to blame for what happened, for why he lunged at me in front of a packed house, in front of all those horrified kids. Maybe I lost my nerve or something in me snapped. I don't know. It was the strangest thing, something that's never before happened to me. In any case, I really fucked up."

He clenched his fist. "I detached from the present moment you see…everything became a blur. I no longer heard the crowds clapping and laughing as the clowns ran through the aisles. Just like that, everyone disappeared. The circus was gone. All that remained was the lion."

"Samson?"

The old man slowly shook his head and smiled sadly. "No…not Samson…No. It was the lion I had killed so many years ago. Back on the private game reserve, I stood face to face with him, those eyes so full of life…seeing him so pure and alive, this surging energy glowing from within, fully aware of his world-in tune with his existence-seeing him in his magnificence…And when he saw me, a knot of fear twisted my gut inside out. I wanted to run like hell, but no. I stood my ground. Lifting my hands to him, I forced myself to step forward. And with each step, the fear began to fade. I just wanted to touch his face and tell him…I don't know. What could I say? *Sorry I blew your brains out? Forgive me?* Ha! Yeah right. I don't think so. Now it was my turn. And as I got closer, his ears perked. He lowered his head and inched forward methodically as if…as if he clearly recognized me as the one...the one who did him in. The hatred glowered in his eyes…smelling my guilt…His eyes shifted sharply from me to the cat of nine tails. Now it was a whole new situation…

'And I knew the situation all too well! No rolling balls or pedestals between us. Nothing…just the bush! And how sweet the smell. I now faced a lion possessed with a wrathful heart central to the landscape of life. I now stood in the midst of his inner elliptical space. His eyes filled with fire…coming to life…senses sharpening as revenge freed him completely."

The trainer looked directly at me and spoke in a very somber tone. "I'll never forget those eyes…like looking into the eyes of the devil himself."

The trainer grabbed his drink and finished it off. "A searing pain throttled me back to my senses though. I was now back in the circus, back in the cage. I heard the crowd screaming, the Ringmaster trying to keep them calm while that god-awful organ music pierced through my ears like a screaming train…

'I lay on my back, my neck and costume covered in blood. Across from me Samson lay on his side, his eyes glazed over looking right at me. Outside the cage stood two triggermen with dart guns aimed prepared to shoot again. I must've suffered a fit of madness...a fit of madness. I don't know how else to explain it. Samson was the one who attacked me, not the one I killed. Both Samson and I were down for good. Witnesses later claimed that I seemed to be in some strange trance. I guess it was the way I walked right up to Samson and tried to touch his face. And well...that's when he went for it."

Again he brought the tumbler to his lips, but it was empty. "Shit."

"So you were hallucinating?"

He stared at me for a while before responding. "Ah hell. Maybe I am crazy."

"No," I said quickly.

The old man guffawed. "I'll probably get canned. The boss man even told me to see a shrink."

"I don't think you're crazy."

He waved me off. "Someone once told me that sanity is imperfection. I still don't know what to make of that but those words have stayed with me ever since..."

His expression stiffened as he leaned in and whispered..."Something must be done about Samson."

There was an unsettling tone by how he said that which left me speechless.

He next reached into his back pocket for his wallet. He placed a few bills on the bar and Tinker came by with a smile. "I'll get your change."

The old man remained quiet staring at the picture. Noticing a strange look on his face, I felt reluctant to say anything more. He looked like someone who just received the death sentence. The moment was long and silent.

Finally, Tinker returned with a dollar bill placing it in front of the trainer, who quickly swiped it from the counter-top, stretched it out and looked angrily at the Great Seal.

"Money...Fucking money. It's all about money. What a shitty thing...hey!"

He pointed out the small iconic eye floating above the pyramid. "The eye of God. That's what it means. Ha! What a joke. Fat greedy pigs! Don't be fooled for one goddamn minute. There are only three reasons why any country goes to war..." He ripped a third of the dollar bill away. "Greed!" And he dropped it onto the floor. "And the second reason? Greed!" He ripped the second third of the dollar bill away and dropped it to the floor. "And the third reason? That's right…greed!"

The last strip of his dollar remained between his forefinger and thumb. He held it close to me. "This my friend is our greatest invention and our greatest curse. So many are in denial about the true nature of what defines us. And that, my friend, is money. It defines all things from beginning to end." And he dropped it to the floor.

The old man tiredly shook his head. "There had been a time when the world was truly responsive, when freedom meant something. But let me tell you that tonight *it will mean something*! For tonight there'll be only one kind of freedom…Just you wait and see…Tonight the eyes come to life like never before. I mean that…"

Slipping off his stool, he shoved the Polaroid into his pocket and shook his head.

"The problem is that this chicken shit outfit only sees Samson as a liability…I've tried to convince them that he's not. Idiots! They have no idea what they're doing. Bah! It doesn't matter. This time I won't allow it! Do you understand me? I am not going to allow it…not this time!"

He then turned away and staggered out the door. Subsequently, a sharp metallic object caught the corner of my eye. It came from the seat of the trainer's stool. Taking a closer look, I saw that it was a small gun!

I held my breath and looked to see if he'd be coming back for it. No one else seemed to notice. Tinker had been leaning against the counter watching the game on TV with his patrons. And there was no indication the old man noticed leaving the weapon behind. He still had not returned for it. I cautiously picked it up, which felt natural in my grasp. It felt good, so I immediately slipped it within the folds of my jacket.

What in god's name was this old man doing with a gun anyway? Now much of what he said took on a whole new meaning, especially his parting words...*I am not going to allow it...not this time!*

Allow what exactly? He did call the circus chicken shit. He called them idiots for believing Samson to be a liability. The old man was obviously upset. Maybe the circus wanted the lion destroyed. Maybe that's what the old man could not allow, like in South Africa? He also spoke emphatically about freedom; how it will mean something tonight. That could mean a lot of things coming from someone with a gun. But what did it matter? He no longer

had the weapon. I did. And I felt pretty bad about it.

Yeah, the old man may have been drunk. But from the look in

his eyes, he gave meaning to every word he said.

I then gathered up all three pieces of the dollar from

the floor and stuffed them into my pocket. I had no idea

why I did that, but nausea struck with such virulence, I

had to make a run for the bathroom.

CHAPTER 6

Once in the stall, I jackknifed over the toilet and let loose. It all shot out like a jet stream from both my nose and mouth. Scotch, beer and whatever else plunged straight into the toilet. After the purging abated, I flushed, staggered to the sink, rinsed my mouth and threw cold water onto my face. I now stared dumbfounded into the mirror. I had to be going crazy. No doubt about it, because the mirror did not reflect my own face. Rather, it was the face of the lion trainer.

I tottered and swayed and reached out to touch the mirror. A physical plane devoid of coherent senses. And when the lion trainer spoke, time became timeless. He repeated that same story about hallucinating in the cage; mistaking Samson for the lion he killed in South Africa. My god. The man was haunted. And that made us both players on the same stage.

I gave in to the mental reruns of seeing Thel appear and disappear like a ghost. She had even frightened me as if she were a ghost. But I didn't believe in ghosts. I didn't believe in a goddamn thing except that she had to be somewhere on this planet. And I'd find her. And I'd feel the coolness of her hand in mine. Meanwhile, the lion trainer had since disappeared from the mirror. Now it was only me.

My eyes were filled with a demented glare. A thin film of perspiration coated my pale skin. And now the fix was in. I even had the lion trainer's gun. And that gave me something to think about.

Just then and without warning, a sharp cramp struck from down below. Oh Christ! Keeping it gripped, I hauled my ass back into the stall, dropped my pants and took a painful shit. Jesus! The cramps were sharp. With all the puking and now this…Why?

After wiping myself, I flushed and went to wash my hands. Abruptly remembering the stolen can of beer in my jacket pocket, I returned to the stall, latched the door, sat down, grabbed the can, cracked it and downed the grog in four large gulps. Soon, my gut filled with gaseous pressure. For a moment I worried I might get sick again. But all that came out were long guttural belches.

A bit relieved, I put the can down and found the gun in my other pocket. I examined it carefully and noticed it fully loaded with eight bullets…Again the words of the old man echoed through my head…

Someone once told me that sanity is imperfection. I still don't know what to make of that but those words have stayed with me ever since

I almost burst out laughing entertaining the idea of blowing my brains out after taking a shit. Yes, my dear old stinky friend. Bless me with imperfection. But what's the use? *Those words*? There are none…just my hand cradling a weapon. No chance I'd do myself in of course, not while looking for Thel. But with a good beer high, I decided to go through the motions anyway…just for kicks. Wondering if it'd hurt much, I shoved the canon against my head and flipped off the safety. Is this what the lion trainer had in mind? Who knows? Who really knows? There were hundreds of possibilities as to why he had the weapon, but I lacked the moxie to speculate further. Although I did feel bad since he probably needed it more than me. I had no use for it…not really. Yet I kept the weapon firmly pressed against my head. It felt good, and I never felt so at peace in my life.

It's true I had already made up my mind not to kill myself, but it was tempting. Up to this point I relied upon a hallucination. And all it did was lead my drunk ass into this bathroom to vomit my guts out, to nearly shit in my pants. And now a gun was pressed up against my head. Brilliant. Who was I kidding? What progress had been made?

Not much. It all became so ass-backwards. I felt like such an utter failure. Thel was nowhere to be found. And this disturbing thought she might be dead crossed my mind.

"She's not dead," I said aloud.

I had to come up with another plan. First, I had to get rid of this gun before it was too late. Maybe I'd just chuck it into the ocean. Already I had lowered the damn thing from my head, flipped on the safety and stuffed it back into my pocket. The best thing was to return to base, take my meds and get some sleep. Hopefully, my head would clear up by morning. I'd be sober. But I also wanted to see my shrink about this amnesia. Somehow, I needed to convince him to help me remember what happened the night before Thel had apparently disappeared. Remembering the whole of that night was key to finding out what happened to her. And the ring had to mean something. She did exist.

I finally stood up and unlatched the door. After it swung open, I froze in astonishment. It was the bathroom mirror...again the mirror…always the fucking mirror.

Thel's eyes-those wondrous eyes-changed colors from gold to silver to watery brown. And those red teardrops were on her cheek too. With a smile, she stood there in the lifeguard tower. Both her hands gripped the rail. She was at a place where we first kissed, where I proposed to her, and where she had disappeared forever! Now it all returned in red; all except her eyes. Yes, those eyes. They just kept changing colors, those eyes looking right at me. Those eyes wouldn't stop changing. They just wouldn't stop.

Curiously, the urge to laugh overwhelmed me. I couldn't contain it. The laughter poured out with uncontrollable spasms. It was an exhilaration of absolute hysteria...and more painful than puking my guts out.

But when somebody walked into the bathroom, I clamped a hand over my mouth. In the attempt to stifle my laughter, it felt like I had just tore my gut in two. Withal, an idea came to mind. I wanted to confirm my supposition about these hallucinations one more time. I had to be sure. I just had to act calm as my rationale continued to float out my ears like a fine water mist.

"Excuse me, sir?"

The young stranger stopped and seemed nice enough, giving me an affable smile. His eyes were mildly bloodshot, but he appeared okay.

I pointed towards the bathroom mirror that had since been reconfigured into an epic pattern of a gorgeous nightmare. "Do you by chance see anything wrong with that mirror?"

He merely glanced at it before giving me a puzzled look. "No. Why?"

I smiled struggling to contain another paroxysm of hysterical laughter. "I'm sorry. It looks warped, like those mirrors you'd see in a funhouse. I prob'ly had one too many."

He laughed. "No worries. We've all been there."

He now moved on to a urinal and began to merrily whistle away. Yup. He confirmed my resolve to return to base, take my medication and get some sleep. For now I continued to battle this ongoing laughing fit while staring at Thel in the mirror. But I knew, with desperate certainty, it was just a mirror. That's all. None of it was real...*none of it*! I should've known all along. No one saw her but me.

I see ghosts hahaha!

But I didn't believe in ghosts. My only belief stemmed from the chance these hallucinations might get worse. And

I'd walk right into a straight jacket without hope of knowing what happened to Thel. I also had to get rid of this gun and fast.

And all this time, the image gave no indication of fading away. On the contrary, the crimson colors became more vibrant than ever. The geometrical dimensions were sharper, presenting the tiniest details, especially in the Dutch design of the tower. Not only did it have a gambrel roof with flaring eaves, but the walls were also covered with baroque flourishes. And the central pediment presented a mermaid flanked by two seahorses. Yes. It was quite an ornamented spectacle for it being only a lifeguard tower. But this was a hallucination after all. And a third dimension took shape. The image itself began to rise above the mirror. It's as if it demanded to be recognized, to be distinguished from the mirror.

"It *is* getting worse," I mumbled, standing directly across from those shifting images.

And that young stranger kept looking at me while washing his hands. He then hurriedly snatched a paper towel from the dispenser and ran out the door. I wondered what he saw. Horror is what I felt. Lavender is what I smelled. So it was pointless to keep on wondering. In any case, I looked back into the mirror.

Beyond the ocular color changes and transfiguration of dimension, I saw something else that bothered me greatly. I knew the mirror was not to be trusted. Yet when I saw Thel's chest rise and fall indolently, as if she were *breathing,* never before had silence been so soundless nor sensation so aroused!

I shut my eyes, shook my head and hoped only to see a reflection, signifying nothing, allowing the moment to pass. Not that my love for Thel had diminished in any way. Absolutely not! Rather, part of the horror was in the delight of seeing her *come to life* in the form of these inexhaustible hallucinations. Unfortunately, that meant the decaying of reason empowering this image to govern my decisions, to dictate my actions, madness fast becoming malignant. That was the horror. Yet my awareness of such madness proved I couldn't be completely crazy, right? A rational madman? A particle of reason did hold its position somehow, encouraging me to keep my eyes closed, to about-face, walk out the door and to stay the hell away from mirrors for good.

But I couldn't do that. I'm sorry. I just couldn't. In the end, my love for Thel prevailed, a love unto its own madness, a disease latched to the soul, the smell of lavender, a warm gentle feeling, and the inability to keep my fucking eyes closed. That's what love did to me. And there she remained looking right at me; breathing like a living creature within the mirror. I slowly approached her. I had to touch that projected symptom of love. I had to see if "she'd" vanish like before, my hand moving closer and closer to the mirror. So what if she did. It was just a goddamn hallucination. But she didn't vanish. She held her place, entirely vivid in her radiance, confined within a self-moving form. In fact, her eyes looked down upon my hand. She seemed to be studying it. Overwhelmed with intrigue, I became perfectly still. Her eyes grew larger, so aware of what was happening, so conscious, so...alive. And I was about to say something to her when...

her hand suddenly sprang out towards mine clearing the glass and breaking into the physical world!

With a startled cry, I leapt back almost falling down.

"Take my hand before it's too late," she said.

My heart froze, the blood in my veins turned cold and I felt a drought in my mouth. My god…Her voice. It sounded so alive. And her hand had the warm color of life. Taking shallow breaths, I slowly backed away from her. "It's all in my head…" I whispered without much conviction. For the smell of lavender thickened in the air. And the walls were closing in. Now a bright flash. Next a roaring ball of fire. Yet Thel never screamed. She never lowered her hand. For the duration, she calmly smiled at me as the flames grew. And the smell of smoke consumed the smell of lavender. Again another flash…and just like that–the mirror was just a mirror…Thel was gone.

CHAPTER 7

She looked calm, so distinct; so gentle. She was on fire. And she smiled at me. She asked me to take her hand for the second time tonight, to take her hand before it was too late. And I didn't. Maybe I never did. And that illuminated the haunting possibility that what she said meant nothing more than a cry for help...to take her hand before she burned to death!

"No!" I barked. "Thel isn't dead. A dream. That's all. Just a dream."

After I ran out of the bathroom, the whole place seemed to sway like a ship being tossed from wave to wave. And in that instant my bum leg gave out causing me to stumble towards one of the barstools. It's then I also collided with someone holding a pitcher of beer.

But right when I began to fall, *this someone* grabbed my arm and yanked me to my feet. He held onto my jacket. His knuckles dug deep into my chest. Next I saw this crazed look on this guy's face. And there was this four-leaf clover tattooed on a pulsating artery wired up his neck. At that moment I realized he was one of the pool players. Great. Just my luck. No bullshit. That's exactly what I thought while looking at his clover tattoo.

"Look what you did, dumb fuck!" he snarled. And the dank smell of beer and cigarettes seeped out his mouth. He leaned in close, pointing out to me his beer-soaked shirt. "You ran right into me!"

I might've apologized if he weren't such a dick about it. Plus he still had my jacket gripped in one hand. A fleeting thought did cross my mind to pull the gun out and blow his head off. But instead, I just told him to fuck off.

His eyes narrowed, and he still didn't let go of my jacket. A second later I heard a sharp whistle from behind the bar. I looked back and saw Tinker glaring at us.

"Cool it," he said, clearing off empty glasses into a gray tub. "Or you're both out.

This fucking maniac finally let go. "We'll settle this outside you sonofabitch."

Now I wanted to kill him. I swear to god I did, especially by how he kept staring me down. It was a stupid stare, yet he probably wanted to kill me too.

"I can't believe I blew that shot," his friend said.

"Fuck that!" the maniac snapped. "Come here, Billy."

Billy swaggered towards us. With that gut of his, he must've weighed close to 300 pounds.

"Goddamn! Look at that scar," he said.

"Fuck that!" the maniac repeated. "Look at my shirt. Look at this. Look what this asshole did."

Billy's head swiveled towards him, examined his shirt, then his head swiveled back to me. "What the fuck?"

The maniac jabbed me in the chest with his index finger. "Outside, fucker."

"Eat shit," I said.

Thereupon he got Red-faced with that wild-crazed look in his eyes. *"Come again?"*

"Eat shit."

It either had to do with the gun in my pocket or of the delirium from seeing Thel in a bathroom mirror that gave me this false sense of courage. In either case, I couldn't keep my mouth shut. I simply couldn't help it and now found myself in a messy situation. Someone was gonna get fucked, except it wasn't gonna be me.

Tinker now walked up with a mop in his hands. He picked up the empty pitcher from the floor, placed it on a table and began mopping up the spilt beer. "Alright fellas. Let bygones be bygones, huh? Accidents happen. The next Pitcher's on the house."

Except it was too late for that. Something in me cracked. And the crack began to spread. It felt profound. Something was about to happen. That's right. Overcome by this brutal sense of humor, I reached into my jacket pocket for the shredded dollar bill and threw all three pieces to the floor. "There you go. Drinks are on me."

Both the maniac and his fat ass friend gazed dumbly at each piece of the dollar fluttering to the floor. Their mouths dropped, and their eyes widened the exact same way at the exact same time. It was all too hysterical. I began to laugh. And when they looked at me with those same stupid expressions, I laughed even harder. My belly ached. They were so goddamn funny. Presently, Tinker had been mopping up the floor with his back to us. Though he turned right around when my laughter escalated.

Billy stepped up and shoved me against the edge of the bar.

But the flaring sting, engulfing my lower back, could

not stop my laughter.

"You're a dead man," the maniac said.

"Alright enough!" Tinker roared, stepping between us. He held up a handful of cash to them. "Take it and go. *Please*!"

The maniac snatched the money from Tinker's hand and turned to me with an odd smile. "We'll be seeing you later, bitch."

Without saying another word, he and Billy turned and walked out. This was too much fun. They did make me feel a whole lot better, much better than throwing back a shot of that 'ol Mescal…polishing the soul with a good shine. Man, they were good!

But alas, the fun was over. The maniac and his fat ass friend were gone.

Tinker looked annoyed, shaking his head. "That was a stupid thing to do," he said. "For your own safety you better sneak out the back. They'll be waiting for you alright. Those dudes seem pretty dangerous. And it ain't nothing to laugh about. I've never seen them here before, but I have enough sense to know you pissed them off good."

"Sorry for all that."

"Just don't ask for another drink. You're through."

He stepped behind the bar, threw the mop down, grabbed a half-filled bottle of Bourbon and served himself a shot. "You nearly got yourself killed."

I nodded while thinking the opposite.

He downed the shot and let out a billowing sigh. "Well, I didn't like them much here anyway. They made some of the folks here feel a bit uneasy. Still, I can't blame them *dip-shits* for getting pissed at you."

I saw the wrinkles in his face deepen. "Yup. Anyway, you got a ride?"

"No sir."

"Got far to go?"

"Sorta."

"I'll call you a cab," he said. "Just sit tight."

I noticed the handful of curious stares, the sotto voce and chuckles from the customers. They did seem pretty relieved. But not Tinker. He still appeared troubled by the whole thing. Maybe I did screw up and took it too far.

Who knows? Right or wrong, the trouble did clear my head up; the laughter did anyway. Thus I laid out a few bucks on the bar for spilling the beer and for whatever else I owed. All I could do now was sit it out until the cab arrived. While waiting, I pondered the situation. Tinker was probably right about those bastards waiting for me outside. But rather than give them the slip why not let 'em have it? Just do 'em in. What difference did it make? Thel was gone.

Wait a minute! You have a plan. Remember?

No I don't remember. That's the problem. I don't remember much except seeing Thel go up in flames.

She is not dead.

Gritting my teeth, I restrained a swelling impulse to head out front and start blasting. Sweat now dripped into my eyes and burned them with the film of warm salt. Still, that tiny voice of hope kept me seated on the barstool. I finally did remember the plan having to do with my shrink helping me remember a forgotten night. Yet what if he refused? What next? Get a priest? Great. Perform a miracle. Split Midnight open and let loose those lost memories. Let them fall through like a stream of sunlight. Oh fuck it. A better plan would emerge after I got some sleep.

Tinker now came by and handed me my cane.

"The driver's waiting out back," he said, pointing towards a rear corridor. "Keep going down to the very end past the bathroom. You'll see the back exit."

"Thanks." Now all I had to do was jump into a cab without being seen. That's all there was to it. Howbeit,

as I headed for the back exit a familiar voice called out my name...

"Stanley? Stanley Reader?"

CHAPTER 8

The man who called out my name looked oddly familiar. Dressed in a faded green sports coat, he wore rimless glasses, sported a bushy goatee and his hair was combed straight back. But what truly defined his presentiment was the expressive surprise in his voice. All of a sudden it hit me... I recognized him at last!

"Professor Miller?"

He was my former teacher, who taught European Literature at the University. Not only was Miller's knowledge on this discipline boundless, he also possessed an intense passion that brought the curriculum to life, his animated persona penetrating the digital age with the ancient text. He made it all quite relevant indeed. I also think he had a thing for Jean-Pierre Melville movies. I'm almost certain of it. In fact, I remember there being a poster of *Le Samouraï* somewhere in his classroom. Oh yes of course. How could I forget? That's right! He did show the film linking it to Rimbaud's *Season of Hell,* the way in which both film and poem show how the one thing worse than being alone is a descent into banality chipping away at the soul of man.

Miller had a way about him. He really did, especially by how he creatively taught his classes. So to see him again brought to heart a warm cheeriness.

"It's been awhile," he said.

"Yes," I said, stepping forward to shake his hand.

And as we exchanged handshakes, his eyes darted from my cane to the scar on my face. "Well, it's great seeing you here. Are you leaving?" he asked.

I hesitated. "Ah…Yeah. There's a cab waiting for me out back."

He took a deep breath and cleared his throat. "Oh. I see. Well…"

And we now fell into an awkward moment of silence, his eyes gazing curiously at my cane.

I was happy to see Miller again but felt weary of having to explain my impairments to him along with everything else. I could already predict the disappointment in his face if he were to hear of my enlistment.

Fortunately, no explanation was necessary since someone or something drew his attention away from me.

Looking past my right shoulder, his eyes widened, and a smile sprang to his face. "Over here Emily!" he exclaimed, signaling her with a wave of his hand. Calmly walking up and standing next to him, she looked quite young.

Her hair was tied back, revealing two silver loops, swaying from each ear. Also, she was clad in a green cardigan sweater, blue jeans and Chuck Taylor Converse sneakers. And an apparent cool confidence filled her brown eyes with complete sangfroid, a characteristic similar to what Miller had. It was uncanny.

In addition, her perfume emitted an earthy scent. Maybe Cardamom or Patchouli? And I assumed she was still in high school, since her arms were curled around a textbook and small planner.

Miller gently placed his hand on my shoulder. "This is my daughter, Emily."

She gave me a natural, genuine smile. "Nice to meet you."

"Same here," I said, turning to the Professor. "I never knew you had a daughter."

"Always full of surprises, Stanley. You know that. Anyway, she's finishing up her undergraduate studies and heading upward into the realm of scholarly wonders."

Emily rolled her eyes and gently elbowed her father. "Stop," she murmured, turning to me. "Are you one of his students?"

"Former," I said. "And by the way, for a moment I thought you were still in high school."

I immediately grimaced realizing how stupid that sounded.

But she laughed. "Thanks"

"Now, now," Miller chimed in. "Flattery will get you everywhere. Must you leave so soon, Stanley? I just finished teaching a class and Emily here just finished taking one. You know the drill. Now we're here to wind things down. Join us for a drink…for old time's sake."

He took Emily by the hand and waved for me to follow. I was struck by how this harmonious encounter did move me to a good feeling. I looked at my watch: 21:29 hours (9:29pm). It was getting late. But when I considered staying, the knot in my belly loosened. The desperate need to leave now began to drift away.

CHAPTER 9

So I joined them at a table near the entrance. Straightaway, Tinker came by and shook Miller's hand. "Always a pleasure, professor."

"Good evening, Tinker."

He gave Emily a wink. "Looking beautiful as ever young lady."

"Thanks," she replied with a wry smile.

But when he turned to me, his amiable expression changed to a baleful one. He crossed his arms. "Your cab's waiting for you out back, remember?"

There was this ominous tone in his voice and silence lingered until I planted my cane to get up. Miller cleared his throat. "Sorry Tinker. But is there a problem? Stanley here's a former student of mine."

Tinker cracked a knuckle; his uneasy look remained steadfast. "He's had too much to drink tonight and should leave."

Miller glanced at me with a baffled look. "You probably don't remember him," he said to Tinker. "A while back he used to come here as part of our little 'Roundtable' group?"

No hint of recognition appeared in Tinker's eyes, though he pondered my face with considerable concentration. By and by he released a tiresome groan. "Is that so?"

"Yeah," Miller continued. "And ah...I asked him to stick around. We haven't seen each other in a while. So…"

The lines in Tinker's face softened, but he pointed a finger at me. "No more drinking. Got it?"

"Yes sir," I said.

"You better go tell that cab driver you changed your mind."

Emily jumped to her feet. "I'll do it."

"Oh for god's sake," Tinker said, exasperated. "Never mind. Sit down. I'll do it." He flashed me an irascible look before asking Miller and Emily what they wanted to drink.

Miller requested a Heineken. Emily wanted coffee. I asked for water. Tinker nodded and left.

"Jesus!" Miller laughed. "You don't seem drunk to

me."

"I had a run-in with a couple of jerks. It was stupid. No big deal. No brawl. Just enough of a ruckus to get us all kicked out. They were being assholes."

Both Miller and Emily burst out laughing.

"Well it sure is great seeing you again," Miller chortled. "You damned rascal."

"What can I say?"

"I'll tell you what," Emily said. "Tinker can sure be scary when he's pissed. Wow."

"Yeah. But he has a right to be," I said, demurely. "I sure as hell didn't make things easier for him."

Miller leaned forward. "How so?"

"I was being an asshole too…not towards Tinker but to those two clowns. I just don't like being pushed around is all."

Emily laughed. "Wish we had arrived earlier."

Miller turned to her. "Show him your little boon."

"Sure thing," she said, pulling out a small black bottle from her purse. In red letters it said: 10% Pepper Gel.

"Mace?" I asked.

"Yup," she replied, dropping it back into her purse.

"Oh by the way," Miller said to Emily, "I forgot to mention that Eliot's joining us in a bit."

She rolled her eyes and groaned. "You're kidding, right?" She turned to me. "Eliot's one of his crony students who's probably seen every movie known to man. Get him started and he won't stop. Like my father, he's the quintessential cinephile." She turned to Miller. "The last time we were here you two kept rambling on about that stupid French director."

"Melville?"

"Who else? You guys just wouldn't stop. I don't know what it is with you and that guy. French movies bore me to shit."

"But why?" Miller exclaimed. "You used to watch them all the time as a kid."

Emily guffawed. "And why do you think? Because you made me. God!"

Resigned, her father sighed. "Oh come on. They're not that bad."

"You still have that Melville poster up in your classroom?" I asked.

"Yes he does," Emily said morosely. "Blah!"

Miller waved her off and turned to me with a pleading look. "What do you think, Stanley? You feel the same way?"

"I…ah…"

"Hey isn't that Pegasus around your neck?" Emily asked, pointing just below my chin.

I nodded and quickly tucked it back beneath my shirt.

"Ah yes," Miller sighed solemnly. "Poetical transcendence. I see your love for mythology has not waned?"

"No sir."

"Where did you get it?" Emily asked.

I almost said Thel got it for me but stopped myself just in time. The thing is—I didn't feel up to talking about her right now much less mentioning her name. So I lied and said my mom gave me the necklace.

Emily smiled. "It's beautiful. Your mom, huh?"

"Yeah. She lives in Italy now."

"*Really*?"

"Yeah. She hooked up with some Italian curator a while back."

Miller tilted his head. "Curator?"

"For antiques. They live in Latium, off the coast of the Tyrrenhian sea."

"Nice," Emily said. "You visit often?"

Presently, visits to the European landscape did not come to mind. Christ. I'll be damned if this amnesia weren't getting any worse. So here again when trying to remember a visit to Italy, I stumbled through a dark musky attic where such a memory might be stashed away like an old forgotten painting. But again, maybe such a painting never existed…

"I can't remember."

Miller and Emily exchanged glances, which now made me feel like an ass. Fine. To hell with it.

"I have amnesia," I said, "symptomatic of Post Traumatic Stress disorder."

"You have PTSD?" Miller asked.

"According to my therapist."

He looked at my cane again but with more gravitas. "Do you mind telling us what happened to you?"

Tinker returned with our drinks and placed a basket of Tortilla chips on the table. "Freshly made. Good'n hot. Nuthin fancy but they get the job done. Enjoy." And he leisurely lumbered back to the bar.

Miller took a sip of his Heineken. Emily stirred cream and sugar into her coffee. Not realizing the degree of my thirst, I drained my entire glass of water in one gulp.

After Emily placed the spoon back on the table, she spoke softly. "You don't have to tell us if you don't want to, Stanley." She glanced at her dad. "We can talk about something else."

Miller nodded agreeably.

But I reached into my pocket, fished out my dog tags and tossed them onto the table. "I joined the marines…" I pointed to my face and leg. "And this is collateral damage, but I don't remember exactly how it all happened. Sorry."

Miller swiped the tags off the table and carefully examined them. "Jesus!"

Emily's eyes widened. *"The marines?"*

"Yeah."

Miller sipped a little more of his beer and placed the

tags on the table. "So this explains why you vanished from school. Why Stanley? *Why* did you enlist?"

Here we go, I thought. As predicted, disappointment filled Miller's eyes. It was like the malediction of a bad curse. Now I just wanted to get the hell out of here. Already I tried to come up with an excuse to leave. But before I could stop myself, the answer to his question slipped out between gritted teeth.

"I don't know."

He placed his two fingers on his left cheek in erudite fashion. "What exactly did your therapist say about your PTSD?"

"He wants me on something called Selective serotonin reuptake inhibitors and Xanax…to help with my panic attacks. But I know he only wants me to remember more about the war. He fails to understand I don't want to remember anything about that fuck-...."

I bit down on my lip. "Sorry."

"So you were clinically diagnosed with amnesia or PTSD?" Emily asked.

"PTSD," I said. "Amnesia's just one of many symptoms. But my doctor also says that it has something to do with my head trauma which occurred in Afghanistan."

I winced at the suddenness of sharp pain in each of my hands. I looked down and realized both were tightly curled into fists. My fingernails dug deep into my palms. Shaking them loose, I now craved for the warmth of the morning sun, for the richness of shade and surrounding trees, for the smell of lavender and the silence broken by Thel's mellifluous laughter. No. I really didn't want to talk about the amnesia anymore. The cycle of day and night turned so rapidly these days, turning with such violent energy, I found comfort thinking like a child, refusing to believe all is to be given, only to be taken away later.

And at that moment I noticed how Emily gave me this peculiar look. Then she glanced at Miller. "Let's change the subject shall we?"

Miller awkwardly cleared his throat. "So I take it you never made it to Bristol?"

"Huh?"

"Oh. Please don't concern yourself if you can't remember. It's when I had given you paperwork needed to attend a lecture regarding the Empirical progressions in England. You had really wanted to go. It was a once in a lifetime opportunity with all expenses paid from a grant. I'm just wondering if you ever went."

"Oh yeah," I sighed with a queasy sense of guilt. "That I remember. So sorry professor. But no. I never made the trip."

And a sweeping gesture of my hand drew Miller's attention towards those dog tags on the table. "As you now know why."

"Please Stanley," he said. "You needn't apologize to me. I was just wondering."

Unexpectedly I felt a bit of a spark however distant the verve. "Didn't that lecture also have to do with the commercial slave trading post back in the eighteenth century, how this may have influenced William Blake's work among other Romantic poets?"

"That's correct," Miller said, turning to Emily. "Stanley here was or *is* a burgeoning Blake scholar."

I waved him off having no idea what he was talking about. Instead, what came to mind were those words, those splendorous words…*those* words written on a plain white napkin…the great artist's words written as a message, a message to me from another great artist.

Why a Tongue impress'd with honey from every wind?

Those words...and nothing more to say.

"Better get back to base," I said at last. "It was great meeting up again, Professor Miller."

I turned to Emily. "And it was nice meeting you." But when I reached out to shake her hand, my arm inadvertently pushed Emily's textbook off the table. It hit the floor with a loud smack.

"Oh shit. Sorry about that."

Reaching for it, I noticed the front cover for the first time. A weary looking Napoleon Bonaparte sat on a rock with his sword pierced into the ground.

A madman said it was all a lie.

And when he saw a rock, he sat down to cool the burning in his lungs. He couldn't move. His chest rose and fell in rapid shallow breaths. His temples pounded away, tenderizing both sides of his brain.

*

Placing the book back on the table, I laid it face down. On the back cover were other historical figures. Teddy Roosevelt's ten gallon grin along with George Washington's stone cold stare and Lincoln's stoic disposition. A gallant horse carried George Armstrong Custer while Hitler saluted his marching war machine. There were knights in armor holding swords and shields and Genghis Kahn held a cutter.

"So you're a History major?" I asked.

Emily smiled. "How'd you guess?"

"Why did you bring your book here?" Miller asked her.

"Just need to catch up on a little reading. I'm about to start a research paper on the Battle of Little Bighorn."

Miller made a face. "As in Custer's last stand?"

"Yup."

"Why?" he guffawed. "The guy was nothing but a psycho Indian killer…an idiot."

"I don't entirely agree with that generalization," Emily countered. "There had been one other Indian village he attacked...successfully that is. And he gave specific orders not to kill the women and children. Don't get me wrong, Dad. It's not as if I admire the guy for messing with Indians in the first place. I'm just giving you the facts. As for Little Bighorn, it's true I do have this morbid fascination with how Custer and his battalion were completely annihilated. One can only wonder about the terror he and his men felt upon seeing the Indians press on and close in. There were some reports that a few of his soldiers even shot themselves in the head before falling into enemy hands."

"Jesus," I gasped, feeling a faint wave of nausea. "When did all that happen?"

"1876 in the Montana territories. Government orders were issued to Custer to remove the Plains Indians from there. That's what triggered the battle. But I have an even stronger fascination as to what happened after the battle; what the Indians did to the dead and why."

"Mutilation?" Miller asked.

"Exactly," Emily confirmed. "Custer's men were mutilated-genitals were removed..." And her voice rapidly rose to a stentorian timbre. "They were disemboweled. Noses were sliced off. They were scalped and decapitated… Yes father. Mutilation!"

"Okay, okay," Miller responded hastily. "I get it. Calm down."

At that moment something disquieting caught my attention at the entrance to the tavern. Looking past Emily's shoulder, I saw someone in Marine Corps Dress Blues.

The dark blue blouse had those gold buttons formed into the Eagle, Globe and Anchor. There were also five ribbons pinned to his blouse: The *Good Conduct, the Sea Service, the Purple Heart, the Combat Action and Presidential unit citation ribbon.* He wore the trousers with the scarlet colored stripes (or blood stripes) that honored those marines who died in the Mexican War of 1847. It was symmetrical perfection along with the glossy black shoes. He even had the NCO sword, tucked safely in its black sheath. He also wore the white cover on his head. He had one chevron with crossed rifles that ranked him as a Lance Corporal.

I still couldn't see his face, hidden within the shadow of his white cover. But when he began to walk towards us, the shadow slowly receded revealing familiar features. And then I knew. Seeing his face come out of the shadows, I recognized him instantly…Sloan…It was Lance Corporal Sloan. We served together in the same unit. I remembered him!

"The Indians mutilated those troops believing their souls would walk the earth forever without hope of ascending into the great sky…" Emily continued.

My throat tightened. My mouth went dry; my heart began to pound. But it couldn't be him. No! Impossible. Now a memory flashed right before my very eyes. I saw him dead in blood soaked fatigues, his face covered by the mask of death. And it happened so goddamn fast. Just like that-his life had been sucked into an infernal vacuum, leaving me cradling a dead man's head. No. It just couldn't be him...the memory slowly disappeared, sinking back into the hellish waters of the abyss...It couldn't be him.

"Custer wasn't mutilated though," Emily went on. "Two elderly Cheyenne women stopped a warrior from desecrating his body. Allegedly, they recognized him to be a one-time lover of a relative."

I brought my knuckles to my mouth and bit down to prevent a scream.

"So yeah," Emily concluded. "It's a bit of a gruesome ritual yet the nature of it affirms the Indian's spiritual belief in ghosts...in the supernatural. And that's what fascinates me more so than the battle itself."

Sloan stood right next to her...

And when he put his hand on her shoulder, she turned and looked up right into his face! She seemed to recognize him and sighed glumly. "Oh hey."

"Well there he is," Miller said. "It's about time."

Sloan shook his hand and smiled. "Just got back from the local cinema. They're showcasing some of Kurosawa's films."

Miller's face brightened. "Oh wow! You're kidding."

Emily groaned. "Oh god. Here we go."

My mouth dropped at what now unfolded before my very eyes.

"Yeah," Sloan said. "And I just saw *Hidden Fortress.*"

Miller frowned. "Hmm. Never saw that one. I did see *Seventh Samurai* but don't recall ever seeing *Hidden Fortress*. Was it good?"

"A masterpiece. This Kurosawa certainly has a sharp eye for the metaphor."

"How so?"

"For such an old film…I mean it's a work of art. The visual landscapes are stunning. And the story itself is beautiful. I don't think I've ever seen a movie where greed, politics and war are transformed into poetry. Yes there's this great samurai hero that propels the adventure but it's more about the princess. After being driven out of her kingdom, she begins a journey of self-discovery, of seeing the ugliness of the world for the first time, of seeing how the impoverished suffer and hunger for great fortune, of seeing the animalistic nature of humanity and the struggle to stay alive. And so the princess is affected in a most profound way."

"Wow," Miller said.

Sloan smiled sheepishly. "I wouldn't mind seeing it again if you wanna check it out, professor Miller. It's pretty amazing."

And that was all I could take. Desperately needing to get out, I scrambled from the booth, fumbled for my cane and almost fell in the process. But *Sloan* grabbed my wrist. I now expected to look right into a pallid emptiness, right into those vacant eyes…but no. Instead, a complete stranger stood there with a healthy vibrancy, his eyes brimming with life. He had short black hair, thick and spiked. He sported square, black-rimed spectacles and wore a dark blue pullover sweater with blue jeans. His round green eyes, fully animated, sharpened tightly as he released my hand and stepped back. His mouth hung open. "You alright?"

Miller cleared his throat. "Stanley. This is Eliot, my fellow cinephile…You're leaving already?"

"Yeah," I gasped, rubbing my eyes and looking again just to be sure…But Miller was right. It was only Eliot. Sloan was gone. *Gone, gone, gone.* Ah…so much time wasted.

I grabbed my cane and quickly hobbled towards the exit. Once outside, I sucked in the coastal air, which diminished the shock of seeing Sloan again. From here the sea was silent, but its rotten fragrance strong, strong enough to prevent me from screaming. Cool and damp, that fragrance now brought Thel back to the forefront of my mind. A magnificent feeling arose that told me I'd see her again. I'd see her very soon. Such a feeling as this felt so keen and convincing. I found meaning in it. Somehow in someway, Thel and I would be together again. I just had to remain faithful to a will prompted by hope. Yes, the sea was silent but its rotten fragrance strong.

CHAPTER 10

While gulping down a pocket full of that rotten air, I heard a growling engine rev up to a roar. What followed was the abrupt appearance of a black truck. It rolled to a screeching halt. The passenger door swung open and out jumped that maniac with the clover tattoo. He had a switchblade in his hand.

The blade sprang open as Billy fumbled out from the other side of the truck. He staggered to the front end. "Hurry up, Jack!" He slurred. "Stick him and let's go!"

Jack charged me. I shuffled back and tried to pull out the gun. Instead, I tripped over my cane and fell to the ground. A pain seared up my leg and sliced through every fiber of muscle. Maybe this maniac already started in with the blade. It was hard to tell. But there was no flash point of dripping blood…only the rapid movement of him kneeling down and taking ownership of the moment. With one hand, he grabbed my shirt and pinned me to the ground. With the other, he raised the blade above my chest.

"Who's laughing now, fucker!" he seethed. His eyes glimmered hatefully. And all at once this stark image of a girl, also with a blade, flashed through my mind.

It happened so fast but came together in startling detail. She had thick hair, long and black. And her piercing green eyes burned with that same hateful glimmer. She had a pretty face but no beauty in her expression. Her blade was aimed at my throat, and I had no idea why nor who she was. But she said something. She said it to me. And what she said I failed to remember. Blood poured out from her mouth. She had fallen to the ground. And a faint smile appeared on her face. My God! I could smell a stench. And it burned right through my nostrils.

...horrible. A fetid odor...and the smell of carbon, of sulfur. A village. Explosions.

"Kafir," I whispered, not knowing what it meant.

"Jack, look out!"

Now it all became a blur, a string of images streaming by in rapid succession...

...a spray sounding like aerosol...followed by a scream...
"My eyes!! My eyes!!"
...a knife dropping to the ground; a man covering his face.
"It burns! It fucking burns! Shoot them!"
...a woman yelling..."911! 911! Somebody call 911!!"

108

...the same man running in circles still screaming about his eyes...another man chasing him, his hands flailing in the air..."Get in the truck! Get in the truck! Get in the fucking truck!"

"Shoot them damn you!"

"Too late."

"Get the knife at least."

"Cunt!"

What followed were the screeching sounds of tires and the acrid smell of burning rubber.

A young woman knelt beside me. Dressed in a green sweater, blue jeans and black sneakers, she possessed an elegant nature, her eyes filled with terror. She asked if I was okay.

No...It definitely was not the hateful girl holding the blade. And I told her so. She frowned and gave me my cane. I noticed a small container of mace in her hand, a hand that trembled violently. Her chest heaved up and down in rapid succession.

She took a deep breath before dropping the black container into her purse. "It's me. It's Emily."
Her voice was laced with a raspy hoarseness. Her eyes blinked several times. I finally remembered...

And the palavering of excitable voices spilled out from the bar. Tinker and Professor Miller led the way.

"What happened?" Miller asked.

Emily stood up. "Stanley was attacked by two awful looking men. I maced one of them pretty good. They took off in a black truck."

"I knew it!" Tinker exclaimed, glaring at me. "I knew they'd be waiting for you!" As he went on explaining how the attack resulted from my contentious exchange with those two assholes, how I bumped into one of them spilling his pitcher of beer, laughing at them and so on, the dark mists of terror began to fade. That mysterious girl's face vanished...

...the girl with the blade...

And I wondered if I'd ever be right in the head again. Struck with a mild fit of dizziness, I put down the cane and thrust both hands into my jacket pockets. One hand gripped the weapon; the other held Thel's ring.

"You okay?" Miller asked, his voice carrying the weight of dismay.

"I think so," I said, stretching my leg out on the ground.

"I have something for you," Emily said, pulling my dog tags out from her purse.

"You left them on the table. That's why I came out here looking for you."

"Thanks," I said, taking the tags and stuffing them into my pocket.

Miller cleared his throat. "Stanley. What can we do to help you?"

Right then I heard police sirens howling in the far distance. And every one of Tinker's customers scrambled back into the bar. Only Miller, Emily, Tinker and Eliot remained outside.

"Did someone call the cops?" I asked, panicked.

Eliot pointed towards himself with his thumb. "I did."

"Why?"

"Because I heard Emily scream 911."

I shot her a look.

"Don't you want to report this?"

"No!"

Miller raised his hand and got real serious. "Take it easy, Stanley."

"Goddamn it," I mumbled, overwhelmed with the sudden urge to run. Trying to stand, I felt a pronounced pain shoot up my leg. "Fuck!"

"You shouldn't move," Emily said.

"I need to get out of here!"

Tinker shook his head. "You need to calm down."

"Just get me out of here, *please*!"

"But Stanley," Emily insisted, "You should give the police a statement. You were almost killed for god's sake."

My stomach tightly coiled up like a spring. Yeah. I bet that cop with his little brat-of-a-daughter sure had it in for me. Now what? Let it be known I ran from the law for breaking into someone's truck for a can of beer? And there was this goddamn gun now in my possession.

"None of what happened here can get back to my Commanding Officer," I said. "Don't you see? I can get into some serious trouble. It's just one more thing to deal with, one more thing my therapist will want to break down for the sole purpose of some psychogenic diagnosis. I just wanna get back to base without anymore hassle."

Annoyed, Tinker spat on the ground. "You should've taken that cab when you had the chance."

Eliot walked up to Miller and whispered something into his ear. Miller frowned. "No."

Then Emily proclaimed to have an idea.

Miller sighed. "Pray tell."

"I'll be right back," she chirped, dashing off and rounding the corner of the tavern.

"Now what?" Tinker asked.

Miller stood akimbo and nervously shook his head. "With her it could be anything."

I cleared my throat lacking the courage to look my former teacher in the eye. "So sorry about all this, Professor. I really am."

There was a pause long enough to make me wonder if he'd bother to reply.

"It's okay," he said at last. "We'll do what we can to help you."

Feeling bad for being such an impudent burden, I really did want to get up and go. But I couldn't. So nothing more was said until Emily returned.

"Whoa!" Eliot exclaimed. "Is that her?"

The heavy rumble of what sounded like a diesel engine approached us and rolled up to the curb. It turned out to be one of those classic muscle cars, sleek and shiny and dark blue with a defined vintage look. The grill was black with vertically stacked headlights. On one side were three

small letters: GTO.

Emily jumped out. "Ready?"

"Is that yours?" Tinker asked.

Both Miller and his daughter responded

simultaneously..."Yes."

Miller rolled his eyes while Emily gave him a smirk.

"My heirloom. Right Dad?"

He shook his head exasperated. "Whatever."

"Hurry. Let's get Stanley into the car."

"What do you have in mind?"

"We need to get him out of here. Remember?"

"I don't think this is such a good ide-…"

"Come on, Dad! There's no time."

Miller looked irritated but reluctantly acquiesced to

his daughter's plea. While he and Tinker helped me to my

feet, Eliot opened the passenger door and handed me my

cane. During which time, the sirens were getting louder.

As I settled in, the smell of leather emitted from the

black bucket seats. Adjacent to the console was a silver

knobbed stick shift. After getting behind the wheel, Emily

lightly pressed on the accelerator. The engine erupted to

life with a loud throaty rumble. Then it quickly settled

into a deep, smooth idle. The vibrations were subtle and tight.

"Jesus!" I gasped. "What a beast!"

She looked pensive. "What you're hearing under the hood is a 400 V-8 motor."

Miller walked to the driver side and Emily rolled down her window. He leaned in. "Please call Stanley a cab post-haste. Don't take him back to base yourself, ok?"

"Aren't you coming along?"

"No. I better wait for the cops. Eliot will take me home."

"Ok. But what are you gonna tell them?"

Miller shrugged. "Don't know yet but will think of something."

"Thank you, professor" I said awkwardly. "Nice car by the way."

He gave me a slight nod. "A fixer upper. Take care of yourself, Stanley."

He reached over and we parted ways with a firm handshake.

CHAPTER 11

After we strapped on our seatbelts, Emily took a deep breath and looked into the rearview mirror. "Shit! I see the cops."

Sure enough, the red flash of lights brightened the blackness of night.

"Punch it!" Miller shouted and stepped away from the car.

Emily shifted into gear and we shot forward and made an immediate left turn onto the coastal highway. Her car had sheer power insofar as the torque had me pressed up against the seat.

Soon she shifted down to a steady speed along the highway while monitoring the rear view mirror with alerted concentration. "I think we're in the clear."

"I should say so," I replied. "Your car moves like a fighter jet."

Emily grabbed the gearshift. "My dad installed this three speed Turbo Hydra-Matic. You select the shift point manually."

I shook my head and commented on how her dad never ceased to amaze me.

Emily smiled.

"I never knew he was so into cars."

"Just this one," she said. "He's had it since he was a teenager. It's his baby, but I've convinced him to hand her over. I love this car."

"By the way," I said, "what you did back there was incredible."

Emily didn't respond.

"The way you handled that mace of yours against tho-…"

"Sorry," she cut in. "I don't mean to sound rude, but can we not talk about that right now?"

"Sorry."

"That's alright," she said, switching on the radio. The insouciant vibe of a saxophone and the swinging beat of drums now reverberated from the speakers. So as the music played, I looked out the window to where a massive body of water accompanied us along the highway.

"Have you heard of Jobim?" she asked.

"Don't think so."

"Well, this is him. It's all about the Bossa Nova…Gotta love it."

I listened for a moment. "Yeah. It brings to mind a dark, hazy lounge filled with people dancing along with their martinis."

"*Martinis*? That's funny. I could see that."

"But I like the music."

"Not your typical cruise music but it's calming to me."

I now reached for those dog tags in my pocket. Once in hand, I flipped them through my fingers over and over again. A familiar voice distant yet clear then echoed from...somewhere.

"I hope I have what it takes to be a good soldier. I just don't want to be a coward is all. I don't want to be a wash out."

Sloan. I do remember him telling me that once. Unfortunately, I had no idea where or when he said that, if it was in boot camp or in the field. And when I thought about that, my dog tags slipped through my fingers back into the recess of my pocket.

Turning to Emily, I saw how she had both hands on the wheel, her head moving subtly to the slow tempo of another song. It seemed she'd been transported to a place not meant for anyone else to find. So I leaned back, closed my eyes and listened to the song too. The voice was beautiful yet filled with so much sadness, the lyrics both rueful and poignant. To hear the haunting solitude of a tender voice sing about the end of a love affair made me feel both

118

serene and melancholy. And I started thinking about Thel and our first time at the lifeguard tower...how we climbed the ladder and gazed up at the stars.

There were thousands upon thousands of them, as if an explosion had just occurred. And while the stars continued to shine forcibly against the azure sky, we saw the moon hover above the water, emitting her autumn glow. It was quite amazing. Captivated by it all, we sat together comforted by the nocturnal silence between us. But eventually a conversation seeped in like the vapors of a warm cup of tea, carrying us through a wide scope of interests and personal dreams, rolling along with the waves throughout the night. And somewhere along the way we shared a kiss that changed everything...

When the song ended, my eyes opened with my heart beating furiously. That memory rang like a Belfry, rattling my brain from side to side. Emily soon made a sharp left turn into a gravel parking lot.

Unexpectedly, I felt something odd and heavy slipping out of my jacket pocket. Reaching down, I quickly realized it to be the gun. Jesus! Close call. Heretofore, this gun had been tucked away as naturally as a wallet in my pocket.

After parking the car, Emily sat there gazing through the windshield. "Have you ever eaten here?" she asked, her voice expressionless.

Following her gaze, I saw what appeared to be a two story beach house with dark wooden shingles and a wide porch. Mounted on the weathered roof was a flashing blue marquee that read: *The Waterfront Café.*

It was also advertised as being a patisserie, specializing in chocolate pastries.

The gun fell back into my pocket as I fell back against the seat.

"No," I said.

Emily then expressed the need to use the bathroom.

"I won't take long," she said. "Do you have a cell phone?"

I shook my head. "Not on me."

"Here," she said, handing me hers. "You can use mine to call a cab. I think we're okay here, right?"

I took her phone. "Yeah."

"I'll be right back."

When she opened and closed the door, that saucy scent of food wafted up my nose making my stomach grumble. I considered going in for a bite to eat. But instead, I closed my eyes feeling the exhaustion sink in the way rainwater sinks into a mudcracked house. Drifting off into a light sleep, I drooped my head to one side.

And that's when I was jolted wide awake by the ringing of Emily's phone. The small LCD screen displayed *Caller Unknown.* Without thinking twice, I answered it. "Hello?"

At first all I heard was crackling transmission. A bad connection is what first came to mind. Yet it sounded too much like the transmission that came from the cop's radio back at the QK-Stop. And again there also came to mind the same image of that dead soldier. But this time I knew. I remembered. It had been Sloan all along. In any case, the sound of the transmission didn't last long. It changed or morphed rather into something more eerie. It still sounded like radio transmission but more distant. What's more its pitch would rise and fall as if trying to tune into the right frequency. And it got even more disturbing. The sound now transformed into plasmic crackles like the sound an egg makes when thrown into a frying pan. And it could've been just that except for the fact the sound continued to change. What followed next were muffled bangs. And there seemed to be this distant howl; like a mix between a soprano belting out a one note opera and an air raid siren. That's how it sounded. Feeling the hairs rise on both my arms, I undoubtedly would describe whatever came from the other end of Emily's phone as either supernatural...or hopefully just a bad connection.

But a voice spoke…

"ʀᴇader."

Stunned, I wondered who that was. Apparently, the caller recognized me just by the sound of my own voice. And as if the situation couldn't get any weirder, the pitch of the voice rose and fell…tuning in and dropping out much like a radio wave searching for the right frequency. Yet, the voice did sound oddly familiar.

"Professor Miller?"

No answer except for that ongoing eerie sound of the distant howl. And I gave serious thought to simply ending the call. I couldn't take listening to that sound for very much longer. Bad connection or not, I didn't like it at all.

"Professor Miller?" I repeated.

It had to be him calling for Emily. With the exception of Eliot and Tinker, Miller had been the only one who knew I was with her. There's also the possibility that what I mistook for a voice was just a radio wave. And so settled upon this conclusion, I came quite close to ending the call until the voice returned…

"If any**thing** be very carefu_l

ton**igh**t."

Unable to move, unable to speak, I felt an icy mist crawl up my throat. Too fascinated to hang up, I heard as this voice continued to rise and drop.

"Trust **me on** this, stanl**ey**.

Your life **is in** da**nger**. And

wh**atever** you do, ke**ep off** the

beach.

stay away from the beeeeach,

It's too dangerous."

Somehow, I finally forced out three simple words. "Who are you?"

"semper Fi, devil dog. DO or die."

The line went dead, and I sprang upward almost hitting my head against the roof of the car. I gasped. *Semper Fi do or die* was a Marine Corps. Motto. *Devil Dog* was a sobriquet for Marine. No wonder the voice sounded familiar. No. Not Professor Miller. It was…

"Sloan? HELLO? *Sloan?*"

But the man was dead! Besides all that, much of what he said didn't make a whole lot of sense. The phone call in itself made no sense.

Your life is in danger…stay away from the beach…It's too dangerous.

At that moment I noticed Emily exit from the cafe. She stood on the porch stretching out her arms and looking up into the sky.

I dropped the phone between the seats and took three very deep breaths to clear out the last of the icy mist. "If only it were a prank call," I lamented. "A twisted idea of a sick joke."

Not only did I need fresh air, I now needed a drink. After opening the car door, I felt the cool air pass in as I stepped out.

While I carefully crawled out of the car, Emily rushed over to give me a hand. "Hey. What's up?"

"Need a drink. Need fresh air."

She gave me a look. "You alright?"

I nodded without saying anything.

To help keep the pressure off my leg, Emily placed my hand on her shoulder, my cane enduring the bulk of my weight. "I bet you can use a drink too after all that's happened tonight."

She laughed. "That's probably not a bad idea. So you haven't called a cab yet?"

"No. But if you need to get home, I understand. I'm good here."

Her smile slowly vanished. "A drink sounds good."

*

The hostess led us to a table towards the back by a window facing the the coastal highway.

"Your server will be right with you," she said, placing two menus down and returning to the front.

Emily hung her purse over the backside of the chair and sat down. Once our waitress arrived, she asked if we wanted anything to drink. Emily ordered a glass of Cabernet. I ordered a Scotch and glass of water. The waitress smiled politely and went to place our orders.

The cafe presented a dark yet cozy vibe. The patronage was sparse at this time of night, a little before 23:00 Hours (11:00pm). Only two other tables were occupied. An elderly man sat alone drinking a cup of coffee. He was reading an Ivan Turgenev novel.
At the other table a young couple sat side-by-side sharing a plate of fries. They fed each other and giggled between whispers. I finally recognized them to be the same ones caught up in the throes of love back at Quinlan's.

When Emily asked for her phone, I grimaced and apologized for leaving it in the car. So she excused herself to get it.

"You'll find it between the seats," I said as she got up to leave.

Leaning back, I looked out the window to where a heavy fog hid the beach behind its ghostly veil. I wondered if a certain lifeguard tower also hid behind the veil. Running my hands over my face, I imagined the joy of running across the highway, slipping in behind the veil and finding the tower. Let the sky fall. I no longer cared. No longer was I afraid. The world was crazier than me. Let it come to an end. Just give me enough time to climb the ladder. Give me enough time to reach the top deck and *this time I would take her hand before it was too late*...That's all I now wanted. And that's all I wanted to think about. But it's funny how the mind works, when at times it seems to have a will of its own, when the longer you try to think about all that's meant by an evening mist or morning rain, the mind's determined to drag you back to the cold and damp,
to where...

...you damn near came close to being murdered tonight.
to where...

...Miller's own daughter literally saved your life.
to where...

...a phone call came straight from the grave.
to where

...a conversation took place. And you've been warned.

Tinker was right. I should've taken that goddamn cab when I had the chance. So be it. If I couldn't hide behind the veil could I at least drill a hole through my head and drain out the brutality of the night like dirty oil?

But alas our drinks had been served. Ah well. I'd have to settle for the Scotch for now. And without further ado, I grabbed the glass and drained it in one swallow. The highway was all but clear. Fine. Let the world have its way. But make no mistake, the next time Thel offered me her hand, I would take it. Climbing the ladder meant more to me than a phone call from the grave. And I knew beyond my amnesia and beyond my psychosis that Sloan had been killed in action. And that left only two logical explanations as to the phone call: I either dozed off and had a nightmare or had another hallucinatory fit. And those two theories helped bring about some relief along with the scotch buzzing in my brain.

So no. I had no intent of staying away from the beach. It now became apparent that my need to find the tower outweighed a warning from a chimerical phone call. It was settled. From here Emily and I would go our separate ways. Feeling a calmness swirl in, I grabbed the water and drank that too.

Eventually Emily returned and slid quietly back into her chair. Craving a smoke, I pulled out a cigarette and began twirling it between my fingers below the table.

"Well," Emily said, "I talked to my dad. All's well. He didn't mention you to the cops."

I accidentally broke my cigarette. "What did he tell them?"

"He didn't get into specifics only to tell you not to worry. But he still thinks you should press charges." She paused. "Me too."

I brushed off the tobacco from my lap and stuffed the broken cigarette into my pants pocket.

"Anyway, I told him where we are and that you plan to catch a cab from here after we have a drink. I asked him to join us but he's calling it a night."

Right at that moment the waitress came to ask if we were ready to order. Emily gave me a quizzical look. "Are you getting something to eat?"

"I'm starving."

She rubbed her chin with thumb and forefinger. "Come to think of it, me too."

She then reached for the menu and read through it. "Here we go. I'll have the chicken salad."

The waitress turned to me. I promptly ordered a steak medium and another scotch...this time neat.

The waitress smiled and left.

"So have you been here before?" I asked.

Emily took a sip of her wine and gazed out the window. "I have not."

A few minutes later the waitress returned with my second scotch and poured more water into my empty water glass. I clasped my drink and made a conscious effort not to imbibe my drink in large gulps.

In the Meantime, Emily continued to gaze out the window. A compatible silence had since emerged and settled in with no urgent need for either of us to talk. For me this kind of silence had great value. It happened once before when we were listening to the music in her car. I don't know whether this type of silence meant anything at all. The fact is, I felt comfortable in my own skin with Emily. Strange as it may seem, it felt pretty good.

Eventually Emily did clear her throat, folding her hands and looking at me with a thoughtful expression.

"There is one thing I've been wondering about. Please don't answer if it's too personal. I tend to ask a lot of questions. It's a bad habit of mine, but I can't help it."

But our food had just arrived looking picture-perfect and smelling delectable.

"Wow," Emily said. "That was fast."

She quickly picked up her fork and shuffled her salad around until the white dressing covered both the lettuce and chicken meat. Once her salad fell into place, she dug in with shameless rapidity.

"Okay," she said. "I'm starving. I'll ask you about it later. Once I get some food into my stomach I'll have better clarity. And maybe I won't have to ask you anything at all."

I laughed and grabbed my utensils. Also too hungry to talk, I cut into my steak without delay. The pinkish texture revealed the perfect cut. And we ate away engrossed in our respective repast. So no. We didn't talk much except to express how good our food was. I also drank up what remained of the scotch.

After we polished off our plates the waitress returned and asked if we wanted the dessert special.

"It's a chocolate peanut banana bourbon cake," she proclaimed proudly.

"Sounds good, but I'm stuffed," Emily said.

"Me too," I echoed lazily.

The waitress took our plates and left.

Leaning back to give my stomach some breathing room, I noticed how Emily gazed at me with this contemplative expression.

"As I said before, there's something I've been wondering about."

"Okay shoot."

She cleared her throat. "Your reaction towards Eliot when you saw him earlier…It's like you…I don't know how else to say it, but freaked out! Why?"

Like an ice cube sliding down the back of my shirt, her question had me sitting right up with a straight spine.

I rolled my head back. Trying to articulate an explanation proved impossible. It remained formless and too elusive for words to grasp. Apart from that, I attempted to try anyway, proceeding in a voice, sounding not like my own. "He reminded me of a buddy I served with in the service. His name was Sloan. He didn't make it."

Emily remained attentive, expecting more of an explanation. But I didn't know what more to say. So the pause stretched into a quiet moment. Eventually, she fell back against her chair and finished off her wine. "I'm so sorry, Stanley."

"No need to apologize. But it was like seeing a ghost."

Emily's eyes flashed in a peculiar way. "It's funny you should say that."

"What?"

"You said that it was like seeing a ghost. Do you believe in ghosts?"

I burst out laughing. "Of course not. I just said that as a figure of speech. Why? Do you?"

Emily shrugged. "A friend of mine, Melissa, is a psychology major, with an emphasis in Parapsychology. She's writing a thesis on the paranormal phenomenon from a scientific standpoint."

"*Really?*"

"Yeah. Pretty fascinating. And it's caught my interest. That's for sure."

"Paranormal? As in the study of ghosts?"

"Yup."

"From a scientific standpoint?"

"That's right."

"But how?"

Emily folded her hands on the table. "Well, take psychology for instance. Hallucinations are factored in as part of the research."

My mouth hardened. "Hallucinations? As in the hallucinatory experience?"

"Yes! So you know the term?"

"I learned it from my therapist. He said I might experience them at some point down the road. I think he was right."

Emily looked befuddled. "What do you mean?"

I held my breath and second-guessed myself. But the sudden urge to talk about it superseded my fear of being judged. "I've been having some pretty bad hallucinations tonight."

She blinked. "Really?"

CHAPTER 12

I rolled my shoulders back and cracked a knuckle under the table. "Let's step-back. Let's step-back to when I said Eliot reminded me of Sloan. Not true. It *was* Sloan. I thought so anyway. That's why I freaked out."

"You mistook Eliot for Sloan?"

"I guess. But it was him in uniform, in his dress blues...*like seeing a ghost.*"

Emily leaned back. "Hmm. That sounds like a certain type of ghost."

"What's that suppose to mean?"

She scratched her head. "It's what Melissa would term as the..." She frowned struggling to remember the term. Abruptly her face ignited with spontaneous recovery. "Crisis Apparition!"

I shook my head. "No. What I saw was a hallucination. I told you. I don't believe in apparitions or ghosts or anything like that."

"I understand. But what makes Melissa's research so interesting is that science is applied to help articulate the meaning of apparitions."

"Huh?"

"First off, Melissa says that an apparition-by

definition-can be either human or animal. Although it can be seen, it can't be present physically. The fact is, up to now science hasn't really been able to dissect the enormous scope of paranormal phenomena that's been ongoing since the dawn of man. Now let's talk psychology. Keep in mind the brain is far more powerful than you realize. It does have the capacity to generate the very same episodes similar to a paranormal encounter. It's called a natural phenomenon or more commonly known as…" She nodded towards me. "…hallucinations. And that's where investigators or researchers have to be careful. So yes. Unless they're properly educated with this aspect of the brain, their investigation could be a complete farce."

She paused to drink some water.

"So with the advancement of technology much of this takes place in sleep laboratories with additional computer support. Such a procedure has paved the way to better articulate the nexus between the mind and brain. With proper monitoring, certain symptoms can be scientifically diagnosed as certain disorders-like PTSD-which otherwise can fool the individual into believing a paranormal experience has occurred, except it hasn't."

"Hold on," I said. "Just to be clear on all this.

Your friend's writing a thesis on paranormal phenomenon to *disprove* the existence of ghosts? Because that's what it sounds like to me."

"No no. Hold on. These Parapsychologists do believe the brain does have the capacity to generate highly acute sensory skills. They don't consider these type of skills as disorders but rather..." She shrugged. "...gifts. And that's where your Shamans or mystics come into play, the ones with the vision quests. They might see spirits or identify certain gods based on their respective cultures. Remember what I said about those Indians who mutilated Custer's men? Now we can easily assert, from our cultural standpoint, that what they did was pure savagery. Yet in their culture this was a custom based on spiritual instructions from their Shaman.

'So to properly identify such visions is to separate natural phenomenon or other mental disorders from the high acute sensory skills. What's being worked on presently is how to critically calculate the sensory input of the brain. So even if a ghost appears only in the brain, it doesn't make it any less real. It had to originate from somewhere, right?"

She had my full attention. "Okay."

"Well the hallucinations you've had are based on real-life experiences. Are they not? Your friend Sloan isn't a figment of your imagination, right?"

"True."

"So it's the same with ghosts or even dreams. Jung calls them your personal dreams, based on real-life experiences or problems in your own personal life…" She paused. "Or was that Freud? Oh I forget. But one of them said it."

Impressed, I sat back struck by the image of Thel's hand breaking through the mirror and reaching out to me. And there was the fire, seeing her go up in flames. Was that based on a real-life experience too? I shuddered.

"Stanley?"

"Huh?"

"You okay?"

"Why?"

"You have this really strange look on your face."

But it was too late. The image of Thel on fire remained rooted in my mind for good.

"Where did your friend learn about all this?"

"As part of her research, Melissa joined an organization that investigates or focuses on paranormal research based on scientific study. It was developed hundreds of years ago by people who believed in the paranormal. Melissa calls it this SPR, but I forget what it stands for. She claims it being established back in the 1800s somewhere in London. According to her, a bunch of scientists, philosophers and scholars were involved, studying paranormal phenomena. Scientific methods were developed to determine if certain hypotheses could be supported and studied. Such hypotheses included telepathy, hypnosis, haunts and apparitions, including the crisis apparition and-…"

"Wait," I interrupted. "You mentioned this *crisis* apparition before. What exactly is that?"

"Unlike other ghosts, the crisis apparition isn't bound to any one place like a haunted house if you will. And you'd be familiar with who it is. In most cases, they show up only during a moment of crisis when the witness's life is in danger…"

"Trust me on this, Stanley. Your life is in danger..."

"Bullshit," I muttered, struggling to gather my wits.

If anything be very careful...

Emily sat back. "I'm sorry. You seem annoyed. I guess most people think all that I've told you is a bunch of bullshit. And I know you don't believe in this sort of thing either."

"No, I'm fine," I said, trying to frame my phone conversation with Sloan into proper context before telling her about it.

"You had said something about this crisis apparition showing up when a life's in danger?"

Emily nodded.

Well, that's exactly what Sloan told me...That my life was in danger.

"Hey," she said, looking straight into my eyes. "Maybe it's time to-..."

I interrupted her. "Look I'm not sure if this was a nightmare or another hallucinatory fit but apparently I had a phone conversation with Sloan not more than an hour ago."

Emily blanched. "What?"

"Yes. It happened while I was still in the car and you went to the bathroom. Your phone rang. I picked up and it was Sloan."

"You mean that marine you saw back at Tinkers?"

I nodded.

"The one killed in action?"

I continued to nod.

"Well…what did he say?"

"That my life's in danger."

Emily's mouth dropped. "Really?"

She then rummaged through her purse and pulled out her phone.

"What're you doing?"

"Gonna check recent calls," she said, switching on her phone and swiping at the screen with her index finger.

"Wait a minute. I already told you it had to be either

a nightmare or hal-…"

"When did you say he called?"

I shrugged. "Dunno. About an hour ago?"

Emily's eyes widened, and she looked up at me with an astounded look on her face. Carefully, she handed me her phone as if it were some kind of explosive device.

I took it and saw the last call being at 10:44pm, *fifty-six minutes ago*. The caller had been listed as unknown.

Dizziness struck me hard enough for my hand to grab the edge of the table.

"Did he say anything else?"

I took a deep breath and handed Emily back her phone. "H-he told me to stay off the beach."

"Did he say why?"

"Because it's too dangerous."

"But he didn't explain why?"

"No."

Emily sat back. "So is that it?"

"Not exactly," I said, scratching the back of my head for no apparent reason. "There were these really strange sounds coming out from the other end of your phone."

"What kind of sounds?"

And so I went on to tell her how at first it sounded like a bad connection, how it went from crackling transmission, to the plasmic popping of a frying egg, to muffled bangs, to the eerie sound of radio waves and how the pitch in this one particular voice rose and fell like a radio wave. I also explained to Emily of my initial belief that it might be her father's voice. But when the voice said…

…Semper Fi Devil Dog do or die…

"…I knew it was Sloan."

Emily nodded not saying anything.

"Are such eerie radio waves associated with a crisis apparition?"

She thought for a moment. "Melissa did speak once about electromagnetic waves being associated with all types of ghosts."

"Electromagnetic waves?"

"Yes. Or like you said…Radio waves. Melissa also defines them as projected energy. But our ears aren't designed to pick up on those type of waves…not like sound waves."

"But I did hear that bizarre transmission on your phone. I heard Sloan's voice too."

"Yeah. Come to think of it, Sloan may not fit the profile of a crisis apparition. I mean I never heard Melissa mention anything about a ghost making a phone call."

I almost laughed had she not said the following…

"But I'm not entirely sure. I'd still like to tell Melissa about it if you don't mind."

I laughed anyway. "I can't believe we're having this conversation. Okay so your phone rang. You've got the time stamp to prove it. But I don't think I even answered it. I mean I do remember dozing off. So when it did ring maybe in my subconscious it provoked a bad dream of this weird conversation with Sloan. Or it was just another hallucinatory fit."

Emily nodded but with an uncertain expression on her face. Irritated by that, I rifled off a number of pointed questions in an attempt to prove my point.

"You did say ghosts had to originate from somewhere, right?"

"Yes."

"And that hallucinations originate from real-life experiences, right?"

"That's right."

"So in other words ghosts are nothing more than outward projections of the mind, right?"

"Well..."

"Which really means they're nothing more than hallucinations!"

Emily shook her head. "No Stanley. You missed the point. That's natural phenomenon. Look. I'm probably not explaining it very well. Melissa's the true expert. You'd have to talk to her about it."

"So do you believe in ghosts or not?"

She appeared startled by my question.

"Well? Do you?"

"Yes," she said slowly. "I do."

And as she looked straight at me, I tried to reiterate that Sloan was not a ghost. But the words fumbled from my mouth in their own separate way, expressing not what the mind intended at all. How this happened I do not know. But Sloan's name is not what came out of my mouth. Instead, the name of another had now been revealed.

Emily tilted her head. "Thel? Who's that?"

Great! Thel's name leapt out from my mouth into the Great Plains of the *drame absurde*. This blunder proved to be unavoidable after all. Taking on a life all their own, the words gave way to a secret no longer kept.

But now I wanted to talk about her. I really did. First, I took a drink of water in an attempt to organize my thoughts. "She was my girlfriend," I said, "who disappeared about a year and a half ago."

"Disappeared? Like gone missing?"

"That's just it. I don't know. It's this amnesia. Maybe she just left me. I can't remember. One night we're at the beach. The next thing I remember is waking up the following morning, and *pouffe*...she's gone. So here I am trying to piece it together."

Emily gave me this ambivalent look of puzzlement and doubt. "That's strange."

"And tonight I tried calling, but her phone's been disconnected. She's not even listed."

"What about her parents? Have you tried calling them?"

"Her mom's been out of the picture for years. And her father was a 9/11 victim. Besides that I don't have contact info on any other relative. She never mentioned them...none that I can remember anyway."

"Friends?"

"Again...none that I can remember."

Emily brushed some crumbs off the table and cleared her throat. "Sorry to hear about her dad."

"She didn't talk much about it."

"Can't blame her for that. What about co-workers?"

"Co-workers?"

"Yeah. Have you tried contacting them? Didn't she work?"

"Thel didn't work."

"Oh."

"But she had money. She helped with expenses. She even financed our trip to New York one time. I just never knew how much she had."

"Inheritance?"

I shrugged. "Maybe. Who knows? Never did she have this sense of urgency to get a job. She was an aspiring artist. That's it. And the one thing she could do was paint."

"Maybe she sold her work for money?"

"Don't know."

There was now a lull in our conversation.

"Have you tried the police?" Emily asked, cutting short the lull.

"Why police?"

"Just to cover all your bases. It doesn't hurt to see if there's anything on her. A Missing persons report?"

Giving thought to that possibility, I crossed my arms.

Emily rubbed her eyes with thumb and forefinger. "If anything, there's always the internet. You could find just about anyone online these days."

She then clicked on her phone and asked me to confirm the spelling of Thel's name. I hesitated but went ahead and spelled it out as she thumb-typed it in. Next, Emily asked for a last name. What I told her was exactly what I told the operator earlier tonight. In other words, scripted dialogue:

No last name. Just Thel.

I did further explain to her how it had to do with Thel's father and his commitment to *Blake Romanticism.*

Emily lifted a smile and began a web search on her device. I couldn't help but hold my breath while waiting for her to find and read some kind of headline like...

THEL, A YOUNG ASPIRING ARTIST, FROM NORTH COUNTY, KILLED IN A FIRE. SUSPECTED HOMICIDE. BOYFRIEND STANLEY READER SOUGHT FOR QUESTIONING.

The waiting continued as Emily continued to slide her finger up her phone's screen. And the more her finger slid, the more she shook her head.

"Nothing," she finally said. "Just a software company."

Scripted dialogue.

"...and William Blake's *The Book of Thel*...hmm."
I leaned forward with a stronger need to talk about Thel.

"The night before she disappeared, I proposed to her. But she turned me down. She didn't believe in marriage. She was very non-traditional in that sense. She didn't even want kids." I placed my hand over my forehead. "And we got into this bad argument. Man it was bad. And you know what? It wasn't even about the marriage."

"What was it about then?"

149

I now heard Thel's voice play out in my head…

…What we have is a wild wisdom.   She runs free through a peaceful valley and drinks from a golden spring.
Please don't kill her…

I remembered every aspect of that argument, especially when I laughed at her. That's what triggered the argument. I laughed at Thel. I laughed at her for what seemed to be this ridiculous notion of basing one's own life on a poem. And that's what Thel did by calling what we had a wild wisdom. I laughed at her for that and so couldn't bring myself to answer Emily's question, unable to admit being a downright rotten bastard.

Emily waited for me to answer but all I could do was shake my head from side to side.

"It's okay," she said. "You don't have to tell me."

"Sorry. I didn't realize it would be so difficult to discuss. Let's just say the argument was my fault and bad enough for me to walk home from the beach without her."

Emily placed her chin between thumb and forefinger. "Do you remember her later coming home?"

"No. All I can tell you is that there's been this lapse in memory. The next thing I remember is searching the house the following morning. No sign of her except for her art equipment along with everything else she owned...her clothes…everything. It's as if she never came home that night."

"So what did you do?"

"Another lapse in memory. The next thing I remember is finishing up with school...moving on with my life."

Emily gave me a funny look. "Moving on with your life? Well you must've known what happened to her if you decided to move on with your life, right?"

"I must've."

"And what about all her belongings."

"All were left in place until my enlistment. I donated her stuff along with mine to charity."

"Her art equipment too?"

"Everything."

Emily cast a glance out the window. "Hmm…So it's not as if she vanished or disappeared. You simply can't fully recall the immediate events following the argument due to your amnesia, right?"

"Right."

"There must be a logical explanation as to why she's gone."

…this fire erupted out of nowhere…

151

Each breath I took seemed to release a tincture of self-doubt in the air. "But for now all that's certain is the argument. And that's my last memory of us together. I haven't seen her since…until tonight that is and in much the same way I saw Sloan."

"How do you mean?"

I gave her the fingered quote sign. "Like this *crisis apparition* you keep talking about."

"What?"

"But it's all hallucinatory. *It's got to be* even though I've been seeing her all night. First, there was the incident in my room earlier tonight. It was of this image I saw on my window not long after waking up.

'It was so vivid, so precise. Amazing. And it was her work. I know this because that was her style of art. Thel was gifted."

"What image?"

"It was a self portrait of her standing in this lifeguard tower, the same one where we went on our first date, the same one where I proposed to her, where we spent our last night together…" I paused, gritting my teeth. "There's something else."

Emily remained motionless.

"Just minutes before waking up, I had a dream of that exact same image. But in the dream Thel spoke to me. She told me to *take her hand before it was too late*. I remember her saying that in the dream. And I don't know what it means, if it's suppose to mean anything at all…"

A cry for help?

I squeezed my eyes shut.

"Stanley?"

My eyes flipped back open to an empty glass. "Each time I see her, she seems more alive."

"And you've seen her in other places?"

"Yes. At Quinlan's coffeehouse. At The Qk-Stop. After that, I chased her down the street all the way to Tinkers. And there in the bathroom is where I last saw her before meeting up with you and your dad. She was *in* the mirror. She broke through it. She reached for my hand and again said...*Take my hand before it's too late*…And then this…"

My stomach tightened when I almost broached the fire.

Emily's eyes were wide and focused. "This what?"

I shook my head. "It's all so very disturbing."

The waitress came by with the check. "Just to let you know," she said, "we close at midnight."

I reached into my pocket for my wallet.

153

"I'll pay my bit," Emily said.

"No," I replied, snatching the bill off the table. "It's the least I can do since you practically saved my life tonight."

Emily cracked a smile. "How's your leg by the way?"

"Better," I said, placing the money on top of the bill.

The waitress promptly swooped in and scooped up the money. "You need change?"

"You're all set."

The waitress smiled and walked away for the last time.

"Well," Emily said, "you didn't have to buy me dinner. But thanks."

"No problem."

"Now Stanley. I would like to clarify something about your amnesia."

"Okay."

"From what I've gathered, it seems to be blocking out two main occurrences: Your experience in combat and the circumstances surrounding Thel's alleged disappearance?"

"Yes. That's right."

"And tonight you've seen not one but two apparitions?"

I felt my face twist away like wrapped cellophane. "I don't like the idea of calling Thel an apparition. That would suggest she's dead, right?"

Emily threw her hands up in a defensive posture. "You're absolutely right. I'm so sorry, Stanley. I didn't mean to impl-…"

I held up my hand. "No. It's okay. It's okay. Maybe it is something I should consider. After all, I do want to get to the bottom of this, to learn the truth as to what happened to Thel…"

And the following words came out from my mouth of their own volition. "…even if she were dead."

Emily shook her head. "Let's not think that way."

Through the window, I looked up and saw the seamless cobalt skin of the universe. Soon the image of Thel, surrounded in flames, blocked it all out. "But doesn't it strike you odd that she'd just leave everything behind? *Everything?*"

Emily took a deep breath before she answered. "Yes."

"And I may have continued on with my life but to then enlist in the Marines? To this day I still don't know why I did it, though now there's this gnawing feeling it had everything to do with Thel."

My god!   I was on the verge of confessing all to Emily, the full
extent of the argument, seeing Thel on fire…No.   Not yet…Not yet.
First, there was a question I now had to ask.

"Stanley.   Are you sure you can't remember if she came hom-…?

I interrupted her.   "So d-do you think Thel could be a crisis apparition based on how she's appeared to me tonight? Is it a credible case? Would it be for Melissa? Tell me."

Emily rolled her eyes. "Oh. I don't know. I'm not the expert here."

"But you're quite knowledgeable about this stuff. I'm not looking for an expert opinion. Just tell me what you think."

Emily lowered her eyes. "No. Not a credible case. Don't forget about your PTSD. You've been through a helluva lot. So that's all it is. Also…now don't take this the wrong way but…you have been drinking tonight. And that could impair your sense of reality, which in turn impairs the credence to your case."

"But I was completely sober when I saw Thel's image on the window earlier tonight."

Emily nodded. "True. But it was completely inappropriate of me to call Thel an apparition in the first plac-…"

"No wait…"

"Please don't interrupt," she insisted. "Just listen. Now to suggest that she could be dead was wrong and I totally apologize for that. What you must do is defer to your diagnosis. You're suffering from PTSD. And it seems pretty goddamn bad. You were in combat after all. So the best way to find out what happened to Thel is to continue on with your therapy, okay?"

I rolled my head back and heaved a big sigh. "This amnesia's got me so fucked in the head. If I could just remember everything right now, to know if she's still alive or…"

Emily leaned forward with a look of reassurance. "One way or another you will find out. But you must be patient."

My eyes were glued to Emily's face.

She shifted in her chair. "Sorry. Did I say something wrong?"

"This latest episode of seeing her in the mirror," I said. "She seemed so much more than just a hallucination. I could feel her presence. She actually spoke to me. Her voice sounded real. And the smell of her perfume, the lavender…Christ! There was that too."

Emily's eyes narrowed as she turned away.

"What is it?"

She shook her head. "Nothing."

"*What?*"

"No Stanley. Again I don't want to give you the wrong idea about Thel."

"For Christ's sake. I'm desperate here. What are you thinking about?"

"Alright. But this is just hypothetical. Got it?"

"Got it."

"If Thel were a ghost-and I say *if* with a capital *I F-* the presence you're referring to, including the smell of lavender, could be what we discussed earlier remember? The radio waves? What Melissa calls Projected energy? She also terms it as a type of stimulus like a magnetic field. Thel would actually be interconnected with the physical world which means with you."

"Like a conduit?"

"Ah…Maybe. Look. The one thing I did forget to mention about Melissa is that since joining this organization, she's become a trained investigator in the field of the paranormal and a good one. She'd be better qualified to answer those type of questions."

I cleared my throat nervously. "So when will I be able to talk to her?"

Emily gave me a dubious look. "Stanley…We already discus-…"

I cut in. "Some of what you said about this paranormal stuff does make sense to me. And again there's Sloan to think about. You don't seem all too convinced he's just a hallucination. You've already implied he might be a crisis apparition. And you want to talk to Melissa about him, right? Come on. I'm begging you."

Emily turned her attention towards her wine glass and seemed hesitant to speak. Finally, she slid the glass aside.

"Would you be willing to be placed under hypnosis?"

"Huh?"

"Hypnotherapy. It's highly suggestive so it won't work if you resist the process of being hypnotized."

"You mean it really works?"

"Only if you want it to."

"For what purpose?"

"What do you think? To help you remember what happened the night before Thel vanished."

"*Say what?* Why didn't you tell me this before?"

Emily sneered. "Because you're a skeptic."

"No. I'm ready."

"First thing's first. Melissa would have to conduct the interview in a controlled environment where she could run some tests."

"When?"

She shrugged. "As early as tomorrow."

"That soon?"

And for some reason, Emily seemed to get upset as her eyes dropped towards the table. "She'll do it for me."

I cleared my throat. "Sorry. Did I say somethi-…"

She shook her head. "No-no. It's not you at all. I'm fine."

Per contra, Emily still seemed upset and made that quite clear by how she then looked out the window and crossed her arms. She got real quiet. A bit strange, but I continued to wonder if maybe it *was* something I said, unless it somehow related only to Melissa?

In any case, I was grateful to Emily for opening up the possibility I'd get this interview with Melissa. I had to know what happened and remain hopeful Thel was still alive

Albeit, I remained skeptical about the validity of the paranormal and of hypnosis for that matter. Conversely, I couldn't ignore the growing anxiety of being hypnotized in which those lost memories of what happened that night could be restored...if the truth could be restored. And if the truth brought about an unfathomable tragedy, if I were found to be responsible somehow...let's just say I now decided to keep the gun for a little while longer.

Anyway, the time had finally come. If Emily were able to arrange this interview with her friend, my search for Thel no longer seemed so pointless and out of reach.

While Emily stretched back against her chair, I now decided to once again look at the ring.

Something about it gave me peace of mind. Perhaps it was the way those delicate furrows further shaped the diamond and sapphires into a flower, the furrows of a glistening floret.

"Is that a ring?" Emily asked, snapping out of her brooding.

I turned the case and gave it to her. She hesitated but finally took it with both hands.

"Thel's engagement ring," I said. "See how it's shaped like a flower? The sapphires are the petals; the diamond's the bud."

"Very beautiful."

"It's a family heirloom. My grandmother's wedding ring. Both she and Thel have the same birthstone. They were both September babies."

The image of the stones reflected in each of Emily's eyes.

"I found it in my sea bag earlier tonight. Strange. I haven't seen it since the night I placed it on Thel's finger a year and a half ago…"

Then my voice faded into the silence, while my thoughts drifted into the past. It was the night when Thel yanked at the ring. She tried to pull it off, but it got stuck on her middle knuckle…my grandmother's ring stuck on her middle knuckle...

And while Emily continued to gaze at the ring, something strange happened. The ring seemed to shine more fiercely than ever before. It emitted a pinkish hue and sparkled like a mirror ball. Never before had I seen anything like it. Not only that, but Emily's eyes flashed from the furious reflection of the bright glittering stones. The ring seemed to come to life!

I now realized it was because of some unusual brightness coming in through the window from outside. Lightening? Skylights? A rain of fire? The end of the world? No. It was none of those things. For when I looked out the window, I saw it to be Thel, staring right down at me. Just inches from the plate glass, half her body transformed into this celestial blur, a bright flame swirling in nebulous colors of silver and gold, both dazzling and lurid. Nonetheless, there was nothing more chilling than her ashen stare. She didn't even seem to recognize me. I took a deep breath wanting to point her out to Emily, except nothing happened. Unable to move, unable to speak, I remained spellbound.

She then drifted to the right, her face filling up with a number of creases, deepening and spreading across her face like childish drawings in the sand. She tilted her head, looking down at Emily with a great change of expression, calmness now pouring over her face like fresh water, cleansing away the hollowness of horror, revealing a peaceful smile nestled upon her lips like a bluebird nestled upon the branch of a forest tree.

I was then distracted by the sound of a cell- phone, which drew my attention away from the window.
I looked across the table right as Emily reached out to hand me back the jewel case. Once I took it, she retrieved her phone and scrutinized the caller.

"Melissa," she mumbled.

I looked out the window. And Thel was gone.

Turning back to Emily, I cleared my throat to tell her what just happened.

But she already took the call. "Hey...No, I'm out with a friend...Just dinner...Yes I know it's after midnight. So what's up?...Okay. Hold on."

She grabbed her purse and rose up from the chair. "I'm gonna take this call outside if you don't mind," she said without giving me so much as a glance.

"Okay but-…"

"And yes I'll ask her about setting up an appointment for you tomorrow."

Before I got a chance to respond, Emily already headed for the front door. So be it. The ring no longer had that strange pinkish color. When my fingers brushed over the diamond and sapphires, they felt like nothing more than a delicate formation of stones. No vibrations, no warmth, no pulse…no life.

Iris colors of brown, pupils focused, an optic emergence, the wavelengths of Thel's glare were lively and piercing. A moment later I looked out the window, where the night carved out its own speculations.

She was just outside this window. Yet when thinking about it, seeing half her body wrapped in flames, I did

164

notice something lost in her face, something different in her eyes, not really knowing what exactly. But each of her appearances, tonight, seemed to get progressively scarier, more sinister. And a frightful feeling overcame me that it was because she might really be dead. It gnawed at me now. And I felt this inexplicable urge to throw the goddamn ring away once and for all. It all felt so fucked up, so split in half. The sadness. The frustration.

I snapped the jewel case shut and dropped it back into my pocket. Looking through the window, I saw how the interior lighting revealed the faint reflection of my face. The combination of light and glass produced this optical image projecting my reflection out beyond the window where I floated above the ground, drifting in and out of focus, glimmering like a star. And I almost laughed aloud when struck by the idea that it was me who was the ghost...

Gazing at my reflection, I tapped the window. "...and not Thel."

When my cheeks flared up with a burning feeling, I reached for my cane and slammed it down upon the inlaid planks of the wooden floor.

CHAPTER 13

Walking out of the cafe, I heard the quiet roar of the ocean from across the highway. A dazzling circle of flames and I still felt compelled. That lifeguard tower had to be close. It felt close. Then out of nowhere Emily-in her hot rod-pulled up to the front of the cafe. She leaned across the passenger seat and opened the door. "Get in."

"What?"

"I think we've been followed."

"*Followed?*"

"By those two creeps that tried to kill you. There's a black truck parked in the back lot."

"Are you sure it's the same truck?"

"Not a hundred percent. But let's not take any chances. Come on."

I stumbled down the steps, climbed in and slammed the door shut.

Once I buckled up, Emily put the car in gear.

The engine roared followed by spinning tires and flying gravel. We flew out of the parking lot and Emily turned left on the highway. Her eyes kept shifting from the road to the rearview mirror. "Hopefully it's nothing."

Hand in pocket, I held tightly to the gun.

Emily laughed. "Hell. Since spraying mace in that jerk's face, I'm probably the one they're after now."

"That's what I'm afraid of."

"Ah. Forget it. I'm starting to feel it was nothing after all."

I rolled the window down half way to get some fresh air. Of all the people to get caught up in this mess, it had to be the professor's daughter. Brilliant.

"Melissa agreed to meet with you for an interview. Does tomorrow still work?"

I paused. "Yes."

I now felt too drained telling Emily about *another* episode of seeing Thel tonight. The image of her looking at me through the window was all too horrible. It had to be this ongoing psychosis. That's all.

Emily took a deep breath. "The transit center's close by. I'll just drop you off there. Grab your cab, get back to base, get some sleep, and we'll talk tomorrow. Let's wait until then to discuss all the details of the interview. Okay?"

I sank back into the seat. The lifeguard tower still weighed heavily on my mind.

"And make sure to give me your number."

Suddenly, a sharp bright flash lit up the rearview mirror. Emily flinched.

I looked back and saw *four* headlights brightly shinning through her rear window.

"That sonofabitch has his brights on!" Emily exclaimed. "God! He's right on my ass."

I tried to look past the glare, and finally saw that… "it's a black truck. Shit. That must be them alright."

"Damn it!"

"Press on the accelerator. See what they do."

"No. Can you reach into the backseat for my purse? Get my phone and call 911."

Presently, we were the only two vehicles on the highway, obscured by patches of fog and darkness. The truck veered to the other lane and pulled up alongside us. Once they were abreast, the passenger window began to roll down. However, Emily stepped on the brakes as the truck continued to move forward. Without a moment to spare, she shifted into reverse and turned the car around.

Once we rolled the opposite way, Emily peered into the rear view mirror. "They're turning around too…of course." With a glint in her eye and faint smile, she shifted gears, propelling the Pontiac to 70mph.

"So you want me to call the cops or what?" I asked after grabbing her phone from her purse.

She spoke softly. "Hold on. On second thought let's see if we can outrun them first."

From behind, we heard the high roar of the truck. Looking through the rear window, I saw it approach us at high speed.

Emily downshifted. The car jerked forward as the needle jumped to 85mph. Then she up-shifted once and once again as the needle pushed 90.

I dropped the phone, sat back and grabbed tightly onto the edges of my seat. "Goddamn, you can drive."

"Thanks…"

The raging sound of the truck blared through the back window.

"Been driving this car since I was sixteen."

The needle had since moved past 90-91-92…

The glint in Emily's eye remained, but her smile now changed to a tiny snarl. She gave a nod. "Actually, this might be fun."

The needle increased past 100mph as the road ahead slithered like a snake. The car handled the high speed with smooth control while Emily firmly helmed the wheel with white knuckled fists. The bright glare reflected sharply off her rear view mirror.

The speedometer now showed 110mph as we blew past a stop sign. We were in a 55 mile speed zone. The truck easily kept up from behind.

"Jesus, Emily. This is bad. Really bad. Those guys mean business."

Up ahead were the flashing taillights of another car. Maintaining her speed, Emily swiftly caught up to it.

She grunted. "Watch this." She shifted gears and swerved into the opposite lane. We then shot past the vehicle.

Next we saw the white flashing headlights of another car coming towards us. Emily maneuvered back into our lane with aplomb.

Glowing street lamps helped with the visibility of this desolate road as we maintained high velocity. And all the multi colored-lit shops vaporized into blurry lightning streaks. There also whistled the wind through the open window. And a strange look appeared on Emily's face, presenting an odd smile revealing many of her teeth.

"I have an idea," she said. "Brace yourself."

She jerked the car into the opposite lane again and slammed on the brakes. We both flew forward as our seatbelts locked into position. The truck rolled past us at top speed. Already, Emily maneuvered the car around and turned onto a side street. It led into a dark quiet neighborhood. Most of the houses had their porch lights on. And Emily quickly switched off her headlights while turning down another side street.

"What now?" I asked.

"These streets are like a maze," she said. "From here, I know how to get to the transit center. We'll be there in ten minutes. First I just need to catch my breath."

She pulled to the curb and stopped the car. Shaking her head, she released a billowing sigh. "Wow! That was fucking wild." She felt her chest. "My god! I can't remember the last time my heart raced this fast." She lifted her hand, trembling vigorously. "I can't tell if I'm scared to death or just pumped. I mean…that was such a rush…the speed, the chase. Wow! I'm fucking speed racer, man!" She laughed a laugh that came from deep down, rich and heavy, resonating with a realization she possessed something never before recognized. And I laughed right along with her, laughing until I felt the tears bubble up to my eyes. My sides ached but it felt good. We were both holding our bellies. And it took awhile to catch our breath as the laughter slowly subsided.

Then out of nowhere a sudden burst of white light flooded the car. We both turned back and saw four large glaring headlights bearing down on us. Next I heard a door open and slam shut. The shadow of a human figure ran towards the car.

"Floor it!" I yelled. "Hurry! Go, go, go!"

"Jesus Christ!" Emily exclaimed. "Who are these guys? Don't they ever give up?"

She slammed the throttle into gear and peeled away from the curb. The sudden effect of centrifugal force pressed me back against my seat. It was hard to breath. Emily already had us up to 40mph within seconds. She wasn't kidding about these tiny streets being like a maze. She made a half dozen turns, tires screeching every which way. I had no idea where we were. But in no time, we motored onto the boulevard and made a right turn heading west, away from the freeway.

"Aren't you going the wrong way?" I asked.

"No."

"But-..."

"In case those jerks find us again use my phone to take a picture of their truck. Aim for their license plate too."

I reached for the phone where it had dropped by my feet. "Where's the camera on this thing?"

Emily grabbed her phone from my hand and tapped the screen a couple times. She quickly gave it back to me. "Once you get a clear shot, hit the camera icon at the bottom. See it?"

"Yes."

"Just make sure your finger doesn't block the lens."

"Got it."

Emily sighed. "And they found us. Here they come. Okay. We're not gonna keep running. Get ready to take the picture. Remember. Aim for the plate number. And I know it might be tricky getting a clear shot of a black truck at night. Just do the best you can."

As they came barreling toward us, I positioned the phone to get a clear view of their plate. But as they got closer, their Brights kept flashing.

"Goddamn them!" Emily snapped. "I'm starting to get pissed here. Hurry, Stanley. Take the picture."

But through all that flashing, I noticed…

"They don't have a license plate…Nothing."

"Alright, just get a shot of the truck if you can."

I took about three or four pictures while their brights kept flashing. I sat back down to see what came out on her phone. "Damn them," I mumbled. "Truck's obscured by all that flashing. Does your camera have video? I ca-…"

"Just call 911. And give them a description of the truck. Tell them our location. Tell them these guys are psychos and you need to press charges for attempted murder."

Emily now increased her speed to 55mph. That's when we heard bells.

"Wait!" Emily shouted, excitedly. A few yards ahead there were red lights flashing. It was a train crossing.

The bells clamored. And the red striped railway arms began to lower.

Looking at Emily, she had that strange look again, that weird smile showing all her teeth. Instantly, I knew what she had in mind.

"Oh no," I gasped. "You can't be serious."

"Hang on, goddamn you!" She shouted in a maddened tone of euphoria.

The Pontiac rocketed forward as she pulled the gearshift back and slammed the pedal down. The speedometer rapidly climbed past 85 to 90mph…And right ahead of us the candy-striped railway arms slowly came down. I checked on the truck. It was still tightly tucked behind us as if hitched to the rear bumper. Now they tried to pull around us.

"Oh no you don't, assholes!" Emily laughed maniacally. Again she shifted gears, which lurched the car far ahead of the truck. The railway arms were about to lock in as we heard the sound of the train; its horn blaring with piercing effect.

The truck blasted its horn too, which sounded more like a weary squeal compared to the train's blaring scream. And as we began to cross, an abrupt luminous beam shot through our windows like a ray gun. We froze for just an instantaneous moment as the train's large cycloptic light dazzled us with its bright intense radiance. Then a shock wave rippled up my spine when the train's horn blasted away again-shaking the car windows. Emily jumped from her seat and screamed.

We almost didn't make it. There was a loud thud at the front end of the car. We had smashed through the railway arms. But that didn't slow us down. Once we crossed the tracks, I turned back and saw the truck brake and swerve sideways. Seconds later, the freight train streamed by at top speed blocking out the vision of the truck completely.

Emily brought the car to a grinding stop and stared straight ahead. She sat in frozen immobility, her face pallid, her eyes wide, and her mouth hanging loose. Her chest rose and fell in quick successions. She was gasping for air. I looked back as the train continued to roll past us. With that truck on the other side, we couldn't afford to stay much longer unless…

And I tickled the gun with the tip of my finger.

"Emily," I whispered. "We have to get going. Now's our chance."

She put the car in gear and drove south on the coast highway. She looked dazed, her mouth still hanging loose.

"You okay?"

She nodded but only once without saying a word as we continued to ride in complete silence.

A few minutes later, Emily finally broke the silence. "I thought we were going to die," She murmured. "Are you alright?"

I took a deep breath. "I think so."

"We were lucky," she said. "I swear to god we were lucky!"

"Fucking A," I replied.

Emily glanced at her watch. "One 'o clock. Sorry but I need to pull over."

CHAPTER 14

There was a musky dampness laden with the brine. And a storm seemed to be on the rise. The low rumbling of thunder echoed from a far distance with a fleet of clouds sailing in from across the sky. Abruptly, a sharp dank odor seeped up my nose going straight to my head. I coughed and noticed that Emily had just fired up a bammy. After taking a long drag, she gave me a wink. "Just what I needed."

I laughed.

"Want some?" she asked, holding her breath. "It's good grass. Really good. Here…"

After handing it to me, Emily walked down to the water. Lifting her arms, she tilted her head back and released a languid groan. I took a hit.

Emily was right. The grass *was* good. The smoke, thickening in my lungs, felt good. And after letting out a good long exhale, I sat down and torpidly dragged my cane through the sand. My muscles loosened from my bones. The pain in my leg began to abate, and I wished the sun would hurry and rise to melt away a lousy urge.

A few minutes later, Emily returned and sat down. Taking the bammy from my hand, she took another long drag and slowly exhaled. She offered it back, and I took one more hit. Emily soon finished it off. In silence, we listened to the roaring richness of the waves and watched as they rolled up to shore. This lasted for quite awhile. Then something happened throttling me into a fit of bewilderment. Emily slid up and leaned against my shoulder. Trying to keep calm, I felt my hands get clammy.

"It's getting cold," she said.

"I-It is."

She started laughing. "Oh my god, Stanley. That train horn is still blaring through my head. What if it never stops?"

"It will."

She stopped laughing "It's strange."

"What?"

"I know this will sound kinda corny but…well. I feel like we've met before."

I shrugged. "It's possible."

"Yeah. But I do feel this strong sense of familiarity with you, almost like déjà vu. I don't know. I'm not trying to be melodramatic about it. My dad might've talked about you once, or maybe we took a class together. Who knows? But I…"

Emily guffawed. "Oh god. Forget it! I sound dumb." Then she lay on her back, crossed her arms behind her head and took a deep breath.

"By the way," she said, gazing up into the sky. "I want to apologize for almost getting us killed back there. We came so close. That train came so close. What a stupid thing to do…" She scoffed. "So much for saving your life tonight."

I shook my head back and forth. "Hey man. As far as I'm concerned you did save my life once again. You've got guts, Emily. No doubt about it. The way you left those guys in the dust? Wow! And here we are on the beach *alive* and getting high. No apologies please. It's all good."

Emily smiled. "Well there is one other thing I'd like to apologize for."

"What?"

"For getting moody back at the café when I agreed to arrange your interview with Melissa. Remember that?"

"Yeah I remember."

"She and I are sorta involved."

What? Emily…a lesbian?

Okay so I was stunned. But I did all that I can to remain composed without revealing a reaction. The whole time, she looked at me closely. All I could do was turn away and take refuge looking out to sea. I guess that meant—with a sense of futility—I turned out to be a single-minded asshole after all. That or it possibly had more to do with her being the Professor's daughter…not that it made much difference.

"Does that bother you?"

I shook my head with aggression. "Of course not."

"Believe it or not, people still get weirded out by the whole gay thing. So I wasn't sure about telling you or not. That's why I got a little weird."

"So why tell me now?"

"I don't know. It's ah…I mean…" Emily slowly shook her head. "Just by the way you've been so open to me about Thel. I greatly admire how you feel about her, your love for her, wanting to marry her and how you're going about tracking her down. And I am so sorry by what you're experiencing; those hallucinatory episodes of her and of your war buddy too. So with that being said you don't come across as being shallow."

I hoped she was right about that. I then asked if her dad knew about it.

Emily sighed heavily. "Yes he does. My mom too. It took them awhile to get used to it. But they're okay with it now."

"That's good to know."

"But what does it matter? My relationship with Melissa has pretty much run its course."

"Sorry to hear that."

"No need to apologize. You see…Melissa and I both went into this relationship knowing it wouldn't last."

"I don't get it."

Emily smiled though her eyes carried a somber gaze. "I came out of an abusive relationship with a fella who was very cruel. Not long after that Melissa and I had crossed paths. Keep in mind I'd never been attracted to the same gender before meeting her. And I wouldn't even claim that because my relationship with a horrible monster was so bad that it jolted a reverse in polarity with my sexual preference. In fact, I don't think that could even happen. But I'll tell you this. When Melissa and I struck up our first conversation, it was a conversation that imperceptibly drew us together. And as it turned out she had recently been burned by some cheating skank. So the last thing we both wanted was to dive into another long-term relationship. Rather, what we each needed was a fairy tale, a goddamn fairy tale. I know that sounds stupid but that's exactly what we needed.

'Up until we met, we both felt isolated in our own pain. And we brought a lot of raw baggage to the table. With that being said, our initial conversation was the first glimmer of enchantment."

Emily paused and took a deep breath.

"Soon after, I finally knew what it meant to be treated like a human being, to feel like a woman, to experience passion and tenderness. With her I discovered those things. We were on the same plain, starving for the same desires. And it did feel like being in a fairy tale. It was beautiful. She didn't control me. I didn't control her."

She again paused to expel a tired sigh.

"But later in the relationship we felt a shift. Something changed. There were times we'd look at each other like strangers. It frightened us. After a while we both realized what was happening. As we became stronger, regaining our self-dignity, the fairy tale began to wane. And that was all we wanted. Because of that we finally knew what had to be done. We had to let go. It's not something we talked about. Like I already said, we both knew it wouldn't last. So when the time came we just let it run its course…" Emily closed her eyes for a moment and shook her head. "I mean…" Another pause. "No matter what-we'll always mean a great deal to each other. We'll always be connected.

'Besides, I do miss…I mean…I haven't lost complete faith in the opposite sex."

I swallowed, struggling to cut past the way Emily looked at me when she said that. I now wondered if she all but admitted being the one who wanted out. Not Melissa. All the more sobering was how listening to her made me understand something else.

I took a long deep breath. "What you've just told me pretty much explains what Thel wanted all along."

"What's that?"

"The fairy tale. I guess that's all she ever wanted."

Emily sat up. "You think so?"

I nodded. "She said that Marriage meant motherhood and death…"

"*What?*"

"…about how marriage can suck dry our sense of self, that we can end up losing our identity, our self-dignity. And something about shattered self-esteem."

"When did she say that?"

"After I proposed to her, the night before she vanished."

"When you had that argument?"

It was now my turn to expel a tired sigh.

"Ah yes. The argument. Of all the memories that can't be remembered, this is the one, which managed to escape the maw of my amnesia, the one I'd rather forget most of all. Fuck it. Here goes…"

Looking straight into my eyes, Emily said nothing.

"I laughed at Thel. I ridiculed her. I laughed at some of the things she said. And when she accused me of laughing at her, I tried to deny it. But it was no use. It was too late. Like I said before, she didn't leave me because of the marriage proposal. She knew I was willing to leave things as they were, that we didn't have to get married. But that no longer mattered to her. It was just too late. I did laugh at her. I laughed at how she wanted to base her existence on a poem. I thought it was childish. I regret it now. Always will."

"What poem?"

"She kept referring to this William Blake poem, a poem she had been named after. It was about what Blake termed as a wild wisdom. And Thel claimed that's what we had…this wild wisdom, running free through a valley. She begged me not to kill it. And that's when I laughed. She called me a hypocrite and tried pulling the ring off her finger. But it

186

wouldn't come off because it was stuck, the very same ring I showed you earlier tonight. She also said something about feeding a garden and hearing a nightingale instead of feeding a worm and hearing it cry."

Emily covered her mouth, stifling what sounded like either a laugh or gasp.

"I really didn't know what to do," I continued, "being both so amazed and angry about the whole thing. Finally, she told me to get out. So I did. I left her at the lifeguard tower to struggle with the ring stuck on her finger."

When Emily realized I had nothing more to say, she cleared her throat. "Don't take this the wrong way, but if your relationship with Thel ended because you laughed at her that would be pretty damn silly."

I signalled agreement with a hand gesture, since I already felt something beyond the argument ended our relationship or would explain Thel's disappearance.

"It wouldn't make sense," Emily continued. "No. It's gotta be something more than that…something you can't remember."

…she calmly smiled at me as the flames grew…

"Make no mistake. Laughing at her was cruel. Yes, you'd owe her an apology. If you meant it, I'm sure she'd forgive you. You went primal. That's all."

I gazed at my hands, bathed in the shadow of a moonless night. All Emily did was validate what I already knew. But I thanked her anyway for being straightforward. She didn't respond. There was silence. At which point, I turned to her and noticed how her eyes were filled with this galvanized energy. It's as if she were struck by an epiphany.

"What is it?" I asked.

Emily looked right at me with this transfixed expression on her face. "Stanley," she said quietly. "Have you ever considered…just letting go?"

It took me a moment to process her question. I then felt a flutter in my gut. "You mean of Thel?"

Maintaining eye contact with me, she slowly nodded.

My throat went dry. And when a strange brightness flashed in Emily's eyes, the full roar of the ocean grew faint. I now had this overwhelming urge to kiss her. It's true. It came out of nowhere. I lost all control. And by how Emily looked at me, she must've felt the same way. Without thinking twice about it, I positioned myself to kiss her, my arm brushing up against her breast. I went primal alright, my instincts boiling up with this vicious desire.

"Stanley? What are you doi…"

I kissed her and felt the warm wetness of her lips on mine... until she shoved me violently away from her.

From her expression, I knew right away this was all wrong. The way she stared agape at me, I had obviously messed up. I did mess up! What the fuck was I thinking? No excuse could justify this act of betraying Thel. The way Emily leaned up against me earlier meant nothing. Acknowledging this mutual sense of familiarity meant nothing. Confiding in me her relationship with Melissa meant nothing. Our shared near death experience meant nothing. She even admitted not losing faith in the opposite sex. *And she looked right at me when she said that.* A confession? Invitation? I guess I didn't understand anything except...that she saved my life. No matter. What transpired between us tonight meant nothing and everything. The door had been kicked wide open and slammed shut. In my attempt to walk through it made me shallow after all. And just like that, Emily stood up and brushed the sand off herself. "We should get going."

"Emily wait…"

But she already turned away and headed for the car. Getting to my feet, I sighed dismally and followed behind feeling sick to my stomach. What a crappy feeling to have someone look at you with disgust. Ah forget it. Just forget it! I'm so sick of dwelling on all the wrong things said or done. The value of love. The value of trust. Annihilated in seconds.

Now I wondered if this search for Thel was even worth it. After all, my last memory of her was of how she made me feel like shit too. Maybe she simply ran off to pursue her own goddamn fairytale. She wanted out. Emily wanted out. Boy. Come to think of it they both seemed to have a lot in common.

Once we reached the car, I took a deep breath. "Emily you go on home."

After opening her car door, she looked at me. "What are you talking about?"

"Come on, Emily. After what just happened I feel like sh-..."

She cut in. "What're you gonna do? Stay here?"

That was a good question. I didn't even feel like looking for that lousy goddamn lifeguard tower anymore.

Whatever the case, I figured this to be a better time than any to part ways.

"I'll be fine. And I'm sorry for what it's worth."

She gave me this flummoxed look.

And right at that moment a bitter longing overcame me. No. I never considered letting go of Thel until Emily asked. And when she did ask there was indeed something appealing in how she posed her question. And because of all that did I love Thel any less? Minutes ago that would've been a ridiculous question to ask. But now I was too afraid to answer it. *Confusion;* this obese demon-purple colored and watermelon shaped-not quite able to swallow a sense of reason, but more than willing to shit out a loaf of contradictions. That's how this *confusion* felt all right.

Emily now regarded me with that look of puzzlement and disgust. I didn't stand a chance. Lastly, I had to remind myself that she also happened to be Professor Miller's daughter. No. I never considered letting go until now.

"Let me at least take you to the transit center," she said.

"No. it's okay."

"Look," she said. "I'm not..."

Emily stopped mid-sentence and slid into the car. Next, she leaned across the passenger seat and threw the door open.

"Stanley come here…" I took a step forward and noticed this drastic change in her demeanor. All signs of disgust and puzzlement were gone. Now her face was filled with alarming purpose. Her eyes were inflamed with fear. A tear streamed down her cheek. "You really want me to leave you here?"

Without waiting for a reply, she settled behind the wheel, slammed her door shut, strapped herself in and started up the car.

I was struck with flashed amazement by how quickly an answer came to mind.

No. Not really.

Not only that but the tear rolling down her face, the fear in her eyes, affected me in some curious way. At that instant I realized the time had finally come. The time had finally come to say what had to be said.

With one hand on the door, I leaned in with this growing sense of indifference towards myself. "I do believe Thel is dead."

At this Emily stiffened, with little change to her alarmed expression. "What?"

"In my dream she goes up in flames. In my hallucination, she goes up in flames. She's burning alive. And it must be based on something real. I think I'm responsible."

Emily's voice was deep and quiet. "You mean responsible for her death?"

Overwhelmed with this strange sense of calmness, I slowly nodded my head. "Yes."

Right then I was distracted by the appalling flash of headlights coming right up behind Emily's car. On an otherwise empty road, it was apparent this vehicle moved exceedingly fast. And before we had time to react, it was much too late. We were trapped.

The black truck swerved dangerously close to the GTO and screeched to a stop right in front of the car. "You've got to be fucking kidding me!" Emily cried out.

Both men instantly jumped out of the truck and charged us. Jack took out his switchblade and pointed it towards Emily. "Look what you did to my fucking face, you cunt!"

His whole face was swollen alright, as if it were about to burst wide open at any moment. He had a fat lip, his nose was discolored and his eyes were all but swollen shut. It's amazing he could still see. Whereupon I wondered if this kind of thing normally happened to a person sprayed with mace, or if it were an allergic reaction, or if maybe Emily had something other than mace in her canister(?) or I could've been having another mental fit enhanced by the grass. I guess it really made no difference now.

He turned to Billy and gestured towards me. "Make it quick. Then help me get the cunt. Hurry up!"

Standing outside the car, I immediately slammed the passenger door shut.

"Dead man," Billy said, leering at me. "You're a dead man."

He now reached for something strapped to his right hip. It took a moment before I realised it was a holstered firearm! And that's when I stopped thinking. An awful feeling took hold from down below. A painful burn quickly rose to my chest. Keeping a firm grip on my cane, I took a cautious step back.

"Oh god!" Emily cried from in the car.

Billy began to laugh. "That cute little friend of yours. Whoa! Gonna split her wide open! Nice ass…yeah a NICE ASS! Love them guts."

194

"Get out of the fucking car you cunt!" Jack yelled, plunging the blade into one of her tires. "Shoot that fucker," he said to Billy. "She locked herself in."

Neither of them saw as I furtively slipped the weapon out of my pocket, the cold barrel meeting my fingertips. And for that, I had only one chance.

As Billy chambered a round, I clicked off the safety, raised the weapon and shot him in the chest. The report popped sharply with combustible force as he froze in absolute amazement. A cloud of blood sprayed out from behind him as his face transformed into a mask. His eyes were wide, and his mouth hung open. And without further ceremony, he crumpled to the ground.

The sound of the shot reverberated like the ghostly echo of a death knell. Next I turned to face Jack.

"*What the fuck!*" he screamed, looking at the fresh corpse piled onto the ground. But it didn't take long for him to notice the gun in my hand. He froze. And I heard this sharp clink. His switchblade had dropped to the ground. His hands flew into the air.

He stammered. "I-I…We…It was…We were only…don't…" He started to hyperventilate. His chest heaved violently. He staggered backwards. And his face seemed to further inflate like a balloon. Fear or anger? Hard to tell while his skin stretched and pulled over a distended face.

"Fuck you!" he exclaimed and spat onto the ground. "Shoot if you're gonna shoot."

Right at that moment, a thunderous explosion came down from up above. It startled me into fearful immobility. Lifting my head, I saw the sky morph into a heavy mountanous layer of black clouds. Lightning flashed across the sky.

"Shoot him!" a woman cried out.

Cold raindrops splattered onto my face. A man screamed. Again, I heard the loud boom and detected the acrid odor of carbon. It smelled like war. Then I looked down to see a body lying prostrate on the street. Taking a closer look, I noticed it had no face. Shattered bones and half a jaw protruded from a pulverized cavity. Bluish pink gore and gray matter gently streamed towards the curb.

It appeared as if Jack's face had finally burst wide open. All that remained untainted, not far from the great wound, was the clover tattoo where all his humanity might've been buried.

Instantaneously, a rumbling ignited into a thunderous crack. A powerful incendiary verve revealed to me, in

shattered blindness, old images reborn into new
interpretations.

It happened all so fast…

*The combustible pop transforms into an audible frequency of
distorted transmission. Haunting images are discharged in rapid
disorder from somewhere between lucidity and madness. All
boundaries between reason and passion are destroyed. Laws are
gone; society is out the cage. The internal universe is not
well. And the symptoms will forever leave a scar. Things get a
bit unpleasant. And so many have already died. Now the
sickness. The behemoth has arrived and we'll call it red death.*

"I never left," I gasped. "I've been here all along."

Artillery roared like a furious dragon, amidst sheets
of rain, awakening me from a stupefied spell of being home
again, of catching glimpses of lost memories...of fragments
of reality and fantasies. My god! *I never left.*
Now I had to find cover and fast. It wasn't safe here.

The roar of artillery was so loud it rattled my skull
like a jackhammer pounding through a block of bad fortune.
Concurrently, I covered my ears trying to keep the static
transmission from seeping through my fingers. But another
flash of explosive discharges. And another, and
another…explosions everywhere. So I turned, raised the
weapon into the air, pulled the trigger and screamed like a

madman. A sharp, loud pop ignited as the rancid odor of war seeped through my nose.

"Incoming!" someone yelled.

I struggled through a horrible pain while lumbering forward, almost falling each time.

Somewhere in the distance I saw something in the shadows approach me. After another explosion, the flash revealed it to be that of a lion. It stopped and glared at me with yellow watery eyes. My eyes were drawn to his eyes-*into the eyes of the devil himself!* But it turned and crept away, disappearing within the darkness.

Next I saw an old man, vaguley familiar, standing by the shoreline. He looked right at me, but I couldn't see his eyes. They had this opaque darkness, empty of life-vacant sockets, like a skeleton and he smiled like a skeleton.

"Beware," he said, his tone melodic yet lugubrious. "We all have our own view of freedom. But tonight there'll be only one kind...Just you wait and see. Tonight the eyes come back to life...beware." And he walked away until he too disappeared within the darkness. *Wait a minute!* I knew that man. He was the lion trainer. But no. None of it was real. It was all a trick of the mind...a fantasy that I had been home…and there had also been the vague memory of meeting up with old friends.

And I heard a voice…a voice that kept calling out my name. It was the sound of a woman's voice...Could it be Thel? But it came from so far away…Far off into the distance. Again my mind was playing tricks on me. You see- the war could do that to a person.

CHAPTER 15

RED DEATH

I stumbled and fell to the ground. Next came the deafening, shattering explosions of artillery whistling overhead...A piercing white flash…A sharp, loud boom erupted from behind. Something came crashing down and rumbled like a terrible earthquake. A tree split in half from the impact of high explosive rounds. And the ground was hot!

Smoke rolled in at circular speed while explosions aggrandized into clouds of apocalyptic intensity. I sprang to my feet and ran for cover. Something metallic burned in my hand…a pistol. And that carbon exuded a sharp and smoky stench glued to the air. There was the smell of gasoline in the air and of sulfur too. Next, I heard a scream. Up ahead

I saw my Lieutenant fall to the ground.

I ran up to him and noticed he'd been shot in the throat. He gurgled. There came another combustible pop and he seized up. Blood poured from both his throat and his mouth. He desperately sucked for air. His eyes widened. He exhaled in a raspy cry. His body twitched and contorted. I lifted his head.

But now he didn't move. He didn't breath. Nothing. He just lay there dead amidst the beating of rounds. I never thought of it like this…and wondered if I had made a big mistake about this whole thing. Courage and leadership and salient intelligence meant nothing at all here. To remain composed and sharp made no difference today. There were only the rattling cries of the dying. And the lieutenant had just died right in front of me.

So I kept running and thought about the time I taught Thel how to play chess. It was on a Sunday, and we were at Quinlan's. She had captured one of my white knights and twirled it between her fingers. But what I remember most about that day was how the sun broke through the window and savagely brightened her hair…

A loud burst echoed from behind. Next a bullet whistled right past my left ear…a bullet out to get me.

But I somehow found a safe place to hide. Huddled in the corner of some half destroyed Hookah café, I wrapped my arms around my knees.

Those loud explosions wouldn't stop. I closed my eyes and covered my ears. What emerged from my mind was the image of a carriage-pulled by two monstrous black horses. The galloping of their hammering hooves momentarily drowned out the explosions as the carriage flew past me. It disappeared into the shadows but left behind a sweet floral smell.

"Lavender," I whispered.

"It's your move," Thel said from across the table.

Her two black knights had cornered my King.

"We can call it a draw," she said, her barefoot finding its way up under my pant leg. And within the hour we were tangled up in damp sheets. We were surrounded by explosions. They escalated and Thel laughed. I got excited. And there were more explosions. It lasted for a long time. When it finally stopped, she comforted me with a kiss and asked me a question.

But I couldn't answer because my mouth was sealed shut. How that happened I do not know. With the touch of a fingertip, my lips felt like dried paint on canvass. And a wind crawled up my back.

"Talk to me," she said. "What's on your mind?"

I still couldn't talk. So she decided to go to sleep; I did too. Not long after, I dreamt about this spectral tower, a tower that rose from the ocean until it reached outer space. Panic struck. For some unfathomable reason it frightened me. It became unbearable. Convinced it had to be a nightmare, I tried to force myself awake. But now my eyes were sealed shut too. My mouth would still not open. And at that moment a half-formed creature arose from the darkness. I couldn't make out what it was except for a yellow, watery eye...inhuman. With a hungry look, it spoke…

Praying Mantis, Praying Mantis, this is Charlie One, request fire support, over.

The voice sounded familiar, but when the eye began to glow, I shook my head violently…

Praying Mantis, Praying Mantis, this is Charlie One, request fire support, over.

The eye looked right at me.

I wanted to scream.

Reader! Reader! Are you all right? Hey! Are you all right?

202

And just like that, both my eyes and mouth popped open. The explosions had finally ceased. So did the gunfire. Though my ears continued to ring. Then to my astonishment, I saw a familiar soldier leaning up against the wall. He sat directly across from me. His hair was matted down by sweat. His face, caked with blood and camouflage, had a crazed expression. At last I recognized him.

"Sloan!" I exclaimed. "Goddamn! What the hell are you doing here?"

"In the shit just like you," he said, breathing heavily.

At that point I noticed his flack jacket torn open. It revealed blood-soaked desert fatigues.

"Shit man" I whispered, taking a closer look. "You alright?"

His crazed expression deepened. "Listen to me, Reader! Those Haji nigger fucks are all over the place. Do you hear me? Everywhere! Those fucking bastards have us surrounded. I have the radio and I'm calling in a fire mission. You better run. You better run like hell, because I'm about to light 'em up. Those niggers are gonna burn."

"Wait a minute!" I protested. "What about you? Where's

everyone else?"

He ignored me while studying a small laminated map. Therein he spoke into the receiver. "Praying Mantis, Praying Mantis, this is Charlie One, request fire support, over."

Breezy transmission now poured out from the radio.

(*Response from fire support*): This is Praying Mantis. What're your coordinates, over?

Sloan told them to stand by before he looked at me. "We all got split up. Just a big cluster fuck. Who were you with?"

"1st platoon," I said. "We got annihilated."

Sloan's face darkened as he pointed past my shoulder. I turned and carefully peered through the aperture of the cafe. Sure enough, about fifteen figures slowly emerged into our line of sight. They wore black turbans with face-veils that covered all but their eyes. Each of them slowly moved down the main road of the village. Their clothes were tattered, streaked with dirt and blood. Some wore frayed sandals; others wore combat boots. Some were armed with AK47s, others with grenade launchers, resting on their shoulders. One carried a small blade. Soon they began picking up loose ammo from the ground and stuffing them into their pockets.

"Keep still," Sloan said before calling in the fire mission:

Sloan: Enemy troops in the open. Company-plus sized
       element. -break- Grid: four six four, eight
       five three, over.

Fire support: Roger Charlie One, I copy company
              plus sized element -break- Grid: four six four
              eight five three. Confirm, over.

"You better go," Sloan told me, "before I confirm it. It's a free strike zone here…a death blossom."

"What about you?"

He grimaced and took a deep breath. "Shit," he gasped, wiping sweat from his forehead. His eyes fluttered and closed. His breathing became imperceptible. Only now did I fully comprehend how his human strength and mortal powers were diminishing. And for a brief moment I thought he just died. There was now this…this penetrating silence.

"Sloan?" I said, leaning beside him.

When I shook his shoulder, his head lolled and slumped over. "Sloan!"

He opened his eyes, but dullness seeped over them like

a thin film. He smiled faintly. "Confirm it, Reader," he whispered. "Confirm the strike and get the fuck out of here."

Suddenly, his eyes widened and he grabbed onto my arm. "I hope I have what it takes to be a good soldier. I just don't want to be a coward is all. I don't want to be a wash out. I don't wanna die!" he gasped. "I am not a coward!"

He then vomited hard onto the ground as his eyes rolled up into his skull. An odious stench violently struck my nose. Gradually, Sloan's expression of suffering melted away into a sallow mask. I lifted his head and called out his name. I shook him, checked his heartbeat and his pulse…Nothing. I positioned him for chest compressions but after examining the gaping hole in his left side, I gave up. The wound was too goddamn big. And he lost way too much blood.

Trying to gather my wits, I closed my eyes and took a few deep breaths. My head felt hot and heavily constrained by the pressure of my helmet. Sweat streamed down my face; the putrid stench of vomit assailed my senses. Holding my breath, I finally peered through the aperture and saw those Haji bastards strip the dead of their accoutrements. They placed cartridge belts in careless piles but carefully stacked the M-16 service rifles pyramid style.

Convinced I was fucked, my hands shook uncontrollably, and my chest began to convulse. At this very moment I didn't want to die either. And out of the blue, a line from a poem came to mind. But it was in German and I forgot what it meant...

Od und leer das Meer.

(*Response from fire support*): Charlie One, I copy company
plus sized element -break- Grid: four six four
eight five three. Waiting for confirmation,
Come in Charlie One over.

I looked into Sloan's lifeless face, and the whole place smelled like shit. I began to weep. I was the fucking coward.

Confirm it, Reader...Confirm the strike and get the fuck out of here.

Up to now, I never killed anyone. And I still found it difficult to think I ever could. Besides, the circumstances simply never gave me the opportunity to let them have it. This was my first patrol, and we had been caught in this ambuscade. Everyone ran for cover, but a number of Improvised Explosive Devices detonated everywhere. They annihilated our platoon completely. Rocket Propelled Grenades streamed down from the sky too. Bullets and explosions chased us into the sublime.

Goddamn them all to hell anyhow. Therein strange yet familiar images began to emerge…

Rivers…Trees…Grass…Rocks…mountains…brown horses…crystal buildings…stars…terra cotta faces…parasols…a strawberry mist…teardrops…the Creeping Jenny…a graveyard…

Yes—I in fact knew exactly what all those images meant…

"Thel's painting," I whispered.

All at once another type of anger and horror engulfed me. For if there was one thing more horrifying than war, more horrifying than this present moment, it was Thel's painting. And it's the one thing I never wanted to think about ever again. Not now. Not ever.

"Stop thinking," I murmured. "Stop damn you. Stop. It never existed. It never happened." All in the mind…just a bad dream…a nightmare. That's all it was. Please stop thinking about her painting. Why can't you just stop? But it wouldn't stop. The strangeness of that anger and horror remained. I tried hard not to think, not to think about that horrific yet gorgeous work of art.

I covered my ears and closed my eyes, fighting to keep that image of her painting buried deep within the bowels of my unconsciousness.

Take my hand before it's too late…

"Please not now," I whispered. I want only to think of the mission…of the fire mission.

Instead, what now emerged was this inexorable regret. Her painting was ah too vivid to the mind's eye, however haunting; and I knew what it meant.

"No," I whispered. "Not now."

She could stay in her peaceful valley…and die there.

I shook my head trying to forget all that.

…how Thel's "tiny" hand reached out to me.

"Please stop."

Take my hand before it's too late!

"Won't you ever go away?"

And I saw Thel's "tiny" face one last time enshrouded in a celestial circle of fire.

I began to rock back and forth.

Maybe I hated you all along...

I pulled the pistol from my holster and flipped off the safety.

those "tiny" eyes, rapidly changing colors from the golden radiance of the sun to the silvery rays of the moon, returning to those natural brown colors, glistening with the faintest signs of life.

I chambered a round.

And there were those two "tiny" crimson colored teardrops.

Something shifted from down deep. The anger and horror now became all too powerful. It stirred my soul into a conflagration. My fingers now gripped the barrel. And I was about to shove it into my mouth.

Fire support: Charlie One, Charlie One! This is Praying Mantis.
Waiting for confirmation on company plus sized
element -break- Grid: four six four eight five
three. Do you copy, over? Come in Charlie One

over.

So be it.

Armed with a fully loaded rifle, a pistol, three grenades and a bayonet, I took the receiver from Sloan's hand and confirmed the strike.

Fire Support: Stand by for five round effect.

40 seconds from my mark…"T" minus

39, 38, 37…

I doubled checked the grenades pinned to my flak jacket. Rather than blow my brains out, I decided to wait to be vaporized by the fire mission.

"30, 29, 28, 27…"

And at that moment, a human figure stepped into the cafe. It was the enemy. Breathing heavily, he disregarded the black veil unraveling from his face. His eyes flashed with hateful surprise before leveling his AK-47 towards me. But I already had the pistol in hand and pulled the trigger.

There was a scream…He did shoot off a burst of rounds.

But they ripped into the ceiling once he lost his footing. I shot him under the left eye, but it was the right eye that popped out, the bullet exiting from his right temple.

"3...2...1...shot out...Here come the hounds!"

It was hard to look away from his face. Now he looked like a faded photograph. The one eye remained open. His mouth was open. He lay there perfectly still, and I never felt so alive. My cheeks were on fire. My eyes burned from the flow of tears. Now I couldn't see a thing. And struck by this dizzying sensation, I felt this sharp pounding in my head. Once again I pulled the trigger a few more times. The blurred image of the body jerked from side to side. Not long after that, my momentary fit of delirium got shattered by the whistling sounds of incoming, roaring down from up above. I peered out the doorway and saw a rocket corkscrew down at incredible speed. With a deafening shriek, it impacted into the ground only a few yards away.

I glanced at the man I just killed and no longer did I want to die. Then I saw all enemy fighters running. I switched my rifle to three round bursts. But another explosion rocked the zone. My eyes vibrated. Fearing the next strike might land on my head; I burst through the doorway and also ran. I ran like hell.

I ran right alongside those enemy fighters. We were running like madmen, we were running together and it was hysterical. That's right. We all now ran from Sloan's dreadful fire mission, the one I had just confirmed. In a matter of seconds flying shrapnel struck one man right through his throat. It sliced his head clean off. And as that head spun into the air, his body sagged to the ground.

Another explosion ripped through the ground spraying sand and rocks up into the air. Three more staggered and stumbled, falling to the ground. Another's head exploded right before my very eyes. And a mist of warm wetness coated my entire face. I released an unrecognizable scream and wiped the gore from my eyes. Others were screaming too. We were all screaming, possessed by an incomprehensible fear. No friends or enemies here. It was every man for himself. And just ahead of me another fell to the ground. I noticed how his eyes bulged, as a large piece of metal sank through the middle of his back. It caused his stomach to rupture, spilling his bowels onto the dirt. I looked away and tried to run faster, but it was too late. After the latest in a series of explosions, a mini-shock wave threw me into the air. I hit the ground head-first and felt an excoriating burn shoot up my leg. Molten shrapnel.

My knee was completely covered in blood, rocks and bits of metal. With severe wooziness and nausea, I tried to crawl away, the ringing in my ears deafening. Then my vision blurred, fading in and out…screams fading in and out…thoughts fading in and out until blackness poured in…absolute blackness…in silence…

The next thing I remember was the cool rain, the joy of it wetting my face. And between the clouds, the moon appeared so bright; so close. The fullness of its circumference was sewn into the starless sky far removed from the rain. How magnificent. Yes. How magnificent indeed. Captivated by the wondrous spectacle of infinity, I almost forgot where I was until the burning vapors of carbon struck my nose. The last thing I remember was Sloan on the radio calling in a fire mission. That's it. Now I lay in the middle of a dirt road. When I tried to stand, my left leg erupted into burning agony. And my head felt strange as if my brain fell off its axis. Falling back to the ground, I tried to catch my breath. And it took quite awhile for the burn to fade into an aching throb. Whatever happened, I couldn't remember a fucking thing.

But what really bothered me most of all was this thirst, this dreadful thirst. I checked my canteens. Both were empty. Great. My mouth was parched. My tongue was swollen and felt like sandpaper.

Eventually, I noticed a body lying a few feet away. To see if he had water, I dispensed of extra weight, unclipped my cartridge belt and flak jacket. I kept my rifle strapped to my shoulder. Bracing for the pain, I clenched my jaw, pressed my hands into the dirt and slowly dragged myself towards the body. There did come the burning pain, but it did not overcome my thirst for water.

Getting closer, I discovered the corpse to be that of an enemy fighter. And he did have a canteen strapped to his hip. But when I reached for it, he sharply sprang out at me like a cobra. *He was still alive!* I cried out, feeling something sharp slice across my face. Reaching up, I felt the blood slowly run down my cheek. That fucking Haji nigger sonofabitch cut my face!

Light-headed, I rolled onto my side no longer feeling a lot of pain.

Then I noticed that Haji fuck trying to crawl away. Trembling with rage, I planted the butt end of my rifle into the ground and used it to pull myself up. Trying not to put too much weight on my left leg, I now used my rifle as a makeshift cane. And I easily caught up to him. Only then did I realize, with great astonishment, his right leg had been blown off below the knee. Tattered flesh and shattered bone are all that remained. And if that weren't enough, once his turban fell to the ground, I noticed the "He" was *not a "He"* at all. No. In fact, this rotten Haji fuck was a "She," a she who looked no more than fourteen years of age. My mouth fell open. Her thick black hair fell to her shoulders in tangles. Her eyes burned with alerted intelligence and hatred. Holding the blade up with one hand, she kept trying to back away. Her physiognomy, however, did reveal weariness without much fear and without the apparent expectation to survive. What's more, her hateful eyes held a type of confidence, placing herself in charge of her own destiny; presenting little doubt she had been no stranger to suffering at all. She even managed to sneer at me with a defiant smile.

There was no point in pursuing her now. Interrupted by a sudden coughing fit, she stopped trying to crawl away. That's when she spat up this liver-colored blood. She was dying. But the whole time she held up the blade. Once her coughing subsided, she wiped the blood from her mouth and dropped the blade. Gazing at the ground, she began chanting something in her own dialect...a prayer maybe.

After she fell back, I stepped closer, managed to sit beside her and lifted her head. She remained alive, though her eyes were losing their emanation. The impression of hate and intelligence now fell into a void of mysterious dimension. Yet when she looked at me, that sneer reappeared. *"Kafir,"* she said before closing her eyes for the last time. I took a deep breath and gently lowered her head back onto the ground.

"What the fuck am I doing here?"

Trying not to lose control, I clenched a fist as my eyes gravitated towards her canteen. I snatched it, unscrewed the cap and gulped down the remaining contents. The water was warm but never tasted so good as it did now. By no means did it completely quench my thirst, but it was far less menacing. Now seeing bodies strewn along the dirt road, I shuddered and wondered about Sloan...if he was okay.

I picked up the dead girl's turban for later use. Continuing to use my rifle as a cane, I went from body to body looking for more canteens. Some were empty; others were half full. Once I drank enough to subdue my thirst, I rinsed the turban with a little water and applied it to my cut. I also had to find a place to hide. Unfortunately, more than half the buildings were razed to rubble. Soon enough I spotted a hookah cafe a few feet away. I staggered towards it. There I'd rest a bit before looking for Sloan. Getting the chance to at last gather some perspective, I now felt like a permanent resident in some mystic graveyard. Only pain and hunger told me I still lived.

Maybe the café had food. Maybe there'd be alcohol. But once I walked into the café there was nothing like that, nothing except for the ongoing spectacle of horror. For it was here where I finally found Sloan. And he was dead.

The blood drained from my face.

"This is hell," I murmured, reaching for his hand. It felt stiff and cold. Then I struggled to pull his arms through the straps of the radio. Lifting his body forward, I unclipped the harness and yanked the radio off his back. Thereon I gently laid him back against the wall. "Mission accomplished, my good friend. You burned 'em all." Dismally, the radio was out of commission, damaged by an impressive blow.

These were hellish territories indeed. And the will to keep going was caught within its own inner war…a war between indifference and the will to survive.

CHAPTER 16

A small light flickered from the other end of an alleyway. When I stepped forward the light got brighter, while the storm showed no signs of exhaustion. It's true. Black clouds poured rain onto a world as if trying to wash away the bloody filth and horrid nature of humanity. And a red stream is what flowed between my boots. Thus through it all, that small light continued to flicker. It illuminated the alleyway that appeared to stretch out into wild exaggerated geometric dimensions—like a scene straight out of some German Expressionistic film.

And so I stumbled between the walls of a dead city until I reached the other end. Currently, a gust of hot air swooped down carrying a very sweet odor reminding me of licorice. Now I found myself standing in solitude amidst a vast coastal landscape.

The war had completely vanished!

And the rain did too.

Standing but a few feet away from the ocean, I had no idea where I was...if this were all a dream or a nightmare or death itself. All that remained was this flickering light. And it turned out to be a small fire contained in one of those portable drum shaped fire pits. From it, sparks blew into the air and vanished with a combustible pop. Placed over the fire pit was this tripod frame, with a cauldron suspended between the legs by steel chains. It hovered above the fire pit like a spacecraft as wisps of smoke swirled up between the sparks. And that strange licorice odor seemed to be coming from it. A peculiar feeling arose…

I've seen this set up once before. But when? Where?

Again the faint memory of a painting Thel had created began to take shape. I shuddered and tried not to think about it. How strange that I didn't want to remember it. There was something about it…I don't know. It happened amidst the battle too. I clearly remember how the thought of her painting almost sent me over the edge. And now it was about to happen all over again. But this comforting smell gradually unfolded a naturalistic sense of inward freedom. The faint image of her painting soon vanished, as the memory of a strange night took form, images geared together like a composed plot, each in a given order, beginning with Thel in my room, followed by this and that to almost blowing my brains out, followed by a train coming at full speed, followed by a moment when I forced a lesbian to kiss me and how I later shot two men to death. As for the lesbian, her name was Emily. That's right. I told her everything there was to know about Thel...about the fire. I laid it all on the line but failed to read the message in Emily's eyes. Yet when I looked down at my hands, I now felt like a murderer. Plus, she saw me shoot those two men to death. By god! That's just great. And it all instantly triggered the war back to life, forever seared into my waking consciousness. I soon realized all this occurred but a few hours ago and wondered what Emily now thought of me.

Whatever the case, I remained uncertain as to the difference between being dead or alive. Oh. To hell with it. What did it matter? The will to find Thel seemed to dry up and die, the past, present and future falling away like bits of dried scabs, all lumped together, thrown into the fire to burn away forever. Okay. I still didn't know where I was, but you know what? I really didn't care. It's true. Instead, I felt the rapture of a tremendous joy. Why? Who knows? I'm sure it had nothing more to do than with the symptoms of going completely mad. Ah-ha! But of course. And I loved it! It felt GREAT! Hooray! Madness for the cure. Hooray for the madness! At last I had found a way out, elevated beyond the substance of suffering and reality-whether it was being home or on the battlefield or heaven or hell-I felt great! Somewhere along the way I lost my cane, but the pain in my leg had even disappeared. This sense of exhilaration assured me of my grand escape from the nightmarish existence of war and everything else that may or may not exist. I simply stopped caring about all that, about the boundaries between existence and nonexistence, being and nothingness. None of it made sense, and as a single dreamer it felt wonderful. Maybe I was dead after all.

But when I noticed a blue tent beyond the fire pit, it brought to mind that strange couple from the QK-Stop, the ones who spoke a different language. A truck with Nebraska plates was the next memory, followed by another of two cardboard boxes in the bed of that same truck…

The smaller one was weathered and beaten. Bits of blue canvas sprang out from the numerous rips in the box. There was a picture of a blue tent on one side with the specs written below it: 18' x 10' 3-Room sports tent.

…*another* memory followed of me throwing the door into a menacing face and of me stealing a can of beer…*from that very same truck!*

222

Could it really be them? And if so what were they doing out here

anyway?

My every nerve impulse straight away urged me to make a run for it and fast.

But when I slowly backed away and turned to run, I saw the unthinkable…

My body locked up in complete stupefaction.

"My god!" I gasped, in absolute disbelief. Yet there it stood. There could be no mistaking it.

It was thee lifeguard tower, the very same one I dreamt about, the one Thel sketched on my window earlier tonight, the very same one we had once claimed as our very own. The ghostly little cabin, with its dim windows, stood firmly upon a sandy knoll. The wooden shingles formed a steeped pitched roof, and a black number **3** was painted onto the cement base of the tower. *This was it,* the only place that made any sense to me, the one place where I truly belonged and the place that had eluded my memory all night long. Call it a dream or a sketch, a memory of the past or hallucination, my heart pounded away like a steel drum. And that's when I also heard laughter burst out from behind me.

CHAPTER 17

I quickly turned and saw two shadows standing on the other side of the fire pit. One was tall and stocky, the other short and rigid.

OH SHIT! It had to be them alright.

I tried to run, but instead tripped over my own legs and fell to the sand. "Goddamn it!" I yelled, feeling a sharp pain mushroom up my leg.

The taller shadow stepped forward, the glow of the fire revealing those menacing features. There may have been a remote chance he didn't remember me as the one who threw the door into his face and stole a can of beer from his truck. So far he carried a calm and contemplative expression. Then what caught my attention were these phantasmagorical images on his shirt. But by taking a closer look, I realized it wasn't a shirt at all. No. In fact, it turned out to be an epic tattoo covering up his entire torso.

Across his chest stretched a number of black clouds hovering above a raging sea. Amidst these tumultuous waters a lone figure skillfully maneuvered a wooden craft with only one oar. His ghostly eyes were like white stones – pure and unknown–each surrounded by a small wheel of fire. Overall, his face held a furious expression. And his skin was a pallid hue, exhibiting a skeletal visage, his white hair flowing back like a dull wispy fog. He wore only a loin cloth, revealing a cadaverous body…I finally realized, with great astonishment, that this spectral boatman was none other than Charon, a greek mythic figure who lived in the underworld and ferried souls across the river styx. Presently, something about this epic tattoo conjured up a faint memory. It was of Thel, whose voice rang out with the most chilling clarity.

It was the artwork of Gustave Dore! I couldn't believe it!

I gripped my forhead; trying to remember where and when she mentioned this; if there was anything more she said to ascertain the connection. Again I looked at the tattoo hoping it might help bring about the full scope of this lost memory. But all I managed to remember was that Gustave Dore, a 19th century French artist and engraver, based some of his work on Dante's epic poem, *"The Divine Comedy."* A scene from that poetic masterpiece, which Dore put to canvass, was now perfectly replicated on this guy's skin. Undoubtedly, the French artist's name sprang from the fragmentary memory of Thel's voice. I always knew her passion for art was matched only by her passion for art history. If only I knew where and when she told me about this artist…and why.

Then movement caught the corner of my eye. It was the other shadow that seemed to drift through the air towards the cauldron. And as it got closer, the glow of the fire steadily revealed the shadow to be a girl in a red overcoat. And yes I did recognize her to be the same girl from earlier at the QK-Stop. But now she appeared to be in a trance, her face completely dearth of emotions. Not until she reached the cauldron did a faint smile emerge. She then spoke in that unfamiliar dialect, her intonation brusque. The man looked at her and gave a nod in response. Turning back to me, he smiled revealing large square brownish teeth. Next he reached into his pocket, pulled out a silver coin and flicked it into the air. It spun the whole way up, formed an arch and then dropped towards the ground. Impulsively, I reached out and caught it.

The coin felt heavy in hand. And because of the verdigris, it had to be ancient. It was also difficult to make out the engraving. But soon I recognized one figure to be Dionysos, the greek god of wine and revelry. Right then I knew it to be an Obol, a unit of currency once used in Ancient Greece. The flipside showed the Griffin, a lion with eagles' wings and the eagle's head. The coin had once been used in the obsequies of Greece during the heroic age. In accordance to Greek custom, the deceased is burned on a pyre with an obol under the tongue. Once the spirit exits the body, Hermes-the conductor of the dead-or psychopomp, escorts the spirit to the shores of the river styx to await the arrival of Charon. Only with the coin could the spirit board his boat to be taken across the river to face judgement by the three judges of the underworld- Rhadamanthys, Minos & Aiakos.

I gasped, astounded by the antiquity of the coin. I now reconsidered the meaning of this guy's tattoo and why he tossed me the obol. Maybe he and the girl were true pagans, practitioners of a dead religion. And when I finally looked up, his face had since darkened, his eyes glowering like hot coals. He almost looked like Charon himself, his expression no less ghastly. To make matters all the more strange, the girl had since closed her eyes and raised her arms over the cauldron. She began to chant in a flaring yet amorous tone seemingly ancient yet changeless. For in both hands she held a small bottle filled to the top with a crimson liquid.

Blood? I wondered.

Now an almost unbreakable certainty told me I had definitely seen that bottle once before. But again I failed to make a connection.

And there was that old book in their truck, the book in another language, a book from another place, another time. A book of outdated traditions? Silly tricks? Frightful superstitions? It could've been a book about witchcraft or Necromancing. In any case, these two people now scared the shit out of me!

In accordance to Greek custom the deceased is buried with an obol under the tongue...

And just like that I dropped the obol into the sand. In subterfuge, I checked my pockets for the gun. *Nothing.*

I must've dropped it somewhere along the way.

There was now only an ominous silence, a silence weighing heavily upon the scene, a silence that seemed gorged with mysterious spells and strange whispers. Regaining my footing, I maintained eye contact with a man who continued to glare at me with that same terrible expression. I slowly backed away and cautiously raised my hand towards him. "I'm gonna leave now, okay?"

In an instant, the man's baleful demeanor vanished. No longer did he look so menacing. In fact he almost looked friendly. He now took a deep breath, cleared his throat and spoke in broken English.

"A lion on the loose, okay?"

I blanched. "What?"

His accent was thick, but he did speak clearly. I just didn't get what he meant.

A lion on the loose?

Abruptly, he walked away and stood beside the girl. Closing his eyes, he joined her in that haunting chant. Ad interim, she poured the crimson liquid into the cauldron. Again, their book came to mind. And I remembered the sketch…

…a man and woman kneeling on either side of this small furnace, made of bricks. The man seemed to be praying while the woman poured something into the furnace. She poured it from a small glass bottle!

"That's it," I whispered. "The bottle."

Right before my very eyes appeared the Tableau Vivant of that very sketch. But I had enough. Without further ado, I did an about-face and hurriedly limped towards the tower, just a hair's breadth away from their Faustian ceremony. Of all the places on the beach…goddamn them anyhow.

And with each step taken towards the tower, I felt myself age as my heart thumped wildly. Maybe this wasn't such a good idea after all. This strange and difficult path ended where everything else ended, where I saw Thel for the very last time. And I'd be lying to myself if I didn't expect to see her waiting for me on the upper deck of the tower...Why?

...because I climbed. Withal, once I got to the top—only the wind welcomed me. I thought it over. Give her more time.

For now, I roughly massaged my leg until the cramping in my thigh loosened up. Only then did I notice the cabin door swinging back and forth to the current of the wind.

I approached it cautiously and walked passed the threshold. The floor creaked. A thick muskiness sagged heavily around my nose. And the interior of the cabin smelled wet. The air felt inescapable and sticky. It reminded me of what a catacomb might smell like...an empty one. Strangely, I felt trapped and quickly shot a glance towards the swinging door. What if it slammed shut never to open again? "Like hell," I nervously jeered and rushed out to where the ocean air swirled in and flushed out the remnants of that moist dankness clinging to my nose.

The sound of waves, gently breaking upon the shore, had a calming affect, like hearing the sound of a southern wind soughing thru an orchard of cherry trees. Eventually I looked up into the sky and saw the most amazing thing: A cumulonimbus cloud revealed a small pocket of the sky. And as the cloud began to drift apart, the small pocket stretched out wide enough to reveal a pacific tapestry of stars. They sparkled amidst a very black night. And that's when I smelled it…the lavender.

"Bullshit," I mumbled, not letting it get to me…not this time. Yet I couldn't help but peer over the rail just to be sure…in case I was wrong. But I wasn't wrong. No appearance of Thel accompanied the sensual comfort of her lavender-as it remained.

And I remained with hands gripped to the railing, whilst this gentle wave of dizziness rolled down my head. An acute sense of exhilaration soon followed. It was just like before when I first noticed that…

And ever so slowly…ever so cautiously I turned back towards the cauldron. No longer were those people standing there. Instead, I heard muffled laughter come from inside their blue tent. Apparently, their ceremony had already come to an end. Howbeit, when looking back at the cauldron, I noticed this rose-colored cloud hovering right above it like a balloon. But rather than float away like a balloon, it instead thickened and expanded like something alive!

I wondered if it could be another hallucination. Soon, a dark form appeared within the cloud. It began to pulsate, taking on a will of its own. The motion was fluid yet blurry, like the formless shape of a sea creature just beneath the surface of the water.

I watched as it slowly faded in and out, stretching and collapsing until it re-assembled into a humanlike figure. The soft fuzziness of the image rapidly gave way to the sharp definition of a face that I recognized instantly. Every joint in my body locked up…"Sloan!" I yawped.

He was adorned in his Dress Blues. His gold buttons shined, his trousers and top cover were a brilliant white and his black shoes sparkled magnificently. All his ribbons were pinned to his chest, representing all that he achieved in war from Combat action to the Presidential Unit Citation to the Purple Heart. His face glowed with a soft golden energy. His smile was kind and subtle, his eyes were pensive yet calm.

He stood within a cloud, floating above a cauldron!

"What are you doing here, Reader?" he asked gently. "I told you to stay away from the beach. I told you it was too dangerous. You fucked up."

Astonished, I remained frozen. "W-what…?"

Sloan continued smiling. "So be it. It's not your fault. Besides, you might survive. In any case, since you're here you might as well watch the movie. I think you'll find it interesting. It's called *Thel's Painting*. Enjoy."

He did an about-face, stepped out of the cloud and dissolved. The cloud next filled with the allure of these Daguerreotype- celluloid images, flickering silently, adding a spectral feel to what now became a moving picture within a cloud.

CHAPTER 18

Thel's Painting

With daring courage strengthened by the engagement ring (safely tucked away in his pocket), Stanley packed a blanket, a bottle of red wine and *Da Vida* chocolate into a picnic basket. Thel gave no hint of intelligence concerning his intent to ask her to marry him. Heretofore, she had been led to believe they were going out for only an evening beach-picnic. Already, Stanley predicted this to be an event jumping from one year to the next becoming a cherished memory to last forever.

And so they were on their way to the lifeguard tower on a winter's evening. Because they lived only a block from the beach, it took them no more than five minutes to get there on foot. Not too many people were at the beach during this time of year; only the locals and some die hard surfers.

Amongst these locals were Stanley and Thel who decided to stop to watch the sunset. And as the sun disappeared below the horizon, it seemed to melt away into the sea; the sun's fading rays still illuminating the sky with ruddy, orange streaks.

Thel squeezed Stanley's hand. "It's like a dream."

He took a deep breath and felt his anxiousness slowly melt away with the sun.

Abruptly they heard this commotion come not far from where they stood. They turned and saw this sizable man assembling a blue tent. He seemed to handle it with ease though muttering incomprehensible words under his breath. Across from him a young girl sat beside a portable fire pit, wedged into the sand. She hummed away with a smile on her face. And despite her jet-black hair and black lipstick, her features reminded Stanley of some kind of white flower. He didn't know why. Maybe it was the anemic hue of her skin and delicate bone structure of her face. Herein, she pulled out several small glass bottles from a duffle bag. Each one was sealed and filled with dark yellowish liquid. When she noticed Stanley and Thel looking at her, she gave them a friendly wave and continued humming. Thel waved back.

"What's that all about?" Stanley whispered.

Thel didn't answer.

"And what's with all those bottles?"

"I count twelve," she said.

The guy stopped assembling the tent and gave them a

cold stare.

Thel immediately yanked Stanley's hand. "Come on."

The young girl kept on humming, while the guy kept on staring.

Thel yanked on Stanley's hand again. "Let's get out of here."

And off they ran towards the lifeguard tower. Once they reached it, they both exploded with uncontrollable laughter.

"That was so weird!" Thel chortled in an attempted whisper.

"Very weird," Stanley replied.

She climbed up the ladder and stopped about half way.

She turned towards Stanley, leaned down and took the basket from his hand. After stepping up topside, she placed the basket down and waited for him. Once he joined her, they stood vis-à-vis and kissed.

For Stanley the moment felt too perfect, too magical to wait any longer to propose. But Thel began to laugh and talked about the way that strange man kept staring at them.

She also wondered why the girl had all those little bottles and what they were for. It was then Stanley took the opportunity to pull the ring out from his pocket with delicate maneuvering. Thel had since pointed out a pod of dolphins swimming south along the coastline. "Wow," she whispered. "Look at that."

Stanley remained silent observing the playful way the dolphins breached the water.

"Hey," Thel said, looking at him. "You seem a bit preoccupied. What's up?"

He turned and gazed fixedly into her eyes. Right away Thel's expression changed and appeared to project the context of his thoughts, her eyes becoming alerted with a natural sort of anticipation. Undoubtedly, she clearly knew a turning point was about to unfold.

And in one rapid gesture Stanley clasped Thel's hand and slid the ring onto her finger.

He cleared his throat. "Thel. Will you marry me?"

Her eyes bulged with astonishment. Transfixed by the brilliance of the diamond and sapphires, she gasped. "My God!"

Stanley noticed how the glittering colors reflected in her eyes while the glittering in her eyes reflected everywhere. But when she looked at him, sadness seeped from those very same eyes. Something seemed to be slipping away. That's how it felt for Stanley anyway. And he panicked as her gaze became fixed. Waiting for her to speak, he stood motionless already sensing the delightful or poetic possibilities getting strangled by the long dismal strains of a more irreparable moment.

She took a deep breath, and when she finally spoke-the tone in her voice carried a resolute conviction. "I can't marry you, Stanley." She then lowered her eyes and continued to gaze sadly at the ring. "I'm sorry."

He now felt the crisp, coastal air rip through his skin with what felt like cold sharp teeth. "Why not?"

She looked up into the sky and closed her eyes. "Such an ordeal is a slow death."

Troubled by the urge to push her off the tower, Stanley stepped back. *"What?"*

When tears began rolling down her face, she walked towards the railing. "It can suck dry our sense of self. We'll end up losing our identity, our self-dignity. It disturbs me. Marriage is nothing but a contract filed away with guilt, shame and shattered self-esteem."

"You make it sound so depressing."

"Because it is. It's Emotional bondage…like harnessing a wild wisdom. Wouldn't you rather stand naked with me before the rising sun?"

Stanley made a face without knowing how to respond to that. Then she turned back, ran to him, clasped his hands and fell to her knees. "What we have now runs deep beyond the reaches of some sacred law. What we have *is* a wild wisdom. She runs free through a peaceful valley and drinks from a golden spring. Please don't kill her."

And before Stanley could stop himself, laughter spewed out from his mouth like venom. *"Are you serious?* Come on, Thel. This isn't a Blake poem for God's sake. This is reality. This is our life!"

She released his hand and sprang to her feet. Her face darkened. And her voice came out slowly, her tone filled with seething anger. "I thought you understood me. But instead you laugh at me. You understand nothing. You're no poet. You're a fucking hypocrite!"

Stanley grimaced. "Wait! I'd never laugh at you."

Her eyes sharpened, her index finger pointing at his face. "Oh but you did."

"Wait..."

"*No!* You did," she shouted, now trying to pull the ring off. "If only you had given me the right to say no."

"Okay fine. We don't have to get marri-…"

"Marriage means motherhood and death."

Astounded, he took a step towards her. "You really mean that?"

"I'd rather feed a garden and hear the nightingale, than feed a worm and hear it cry."

Stanley couldn't speak.

"I thought you understood me."

"You'll tear your skin," he said, watching as she tugged violently at the ring.

"I'll get it off."

When their eyes locked, Stanley felt the crushing weight of the night. "We don't have to get married. We'll leave things as they were."

"Get out!" she cried. "Get out of here!"

And she fell back to her knees.

Instead of comforting her, Stanley was paralyzed with his own anger. It struck his chest like a spear, the end point lodged between muscle and bone. It knew more than he did. Right at that moment he remembered a line from the Blake poem from which she was named, from which she now seemed to base her whole entire life...*EVERY THING THAT LIVES LIVES NOT ALONE NOR FOR ITSELF...*

And he almost told her so but didn't. She was too self-possessed, and he hated her. He hated her because she made him feel bad about himself. He hated her because she spoke like a child. He hated her because she was ridiculous. Now all that remained was contempt, eating away at every organ in his body like a black cancer.

"Fine!" Stanley yelled. "Stay in your peaceful valley, drink from the golden spring and die there!"

He glanced at the ring, but it now looked too much like a spider, its fangs embedded in her skin. And he laughed at once. He laughed like a madman. He jumped off the tower like a madman. "It's all a lie!" he screamed and ran off like a madman.

Despite the growing distance between them, Thel's voice overreached Stanley with strident efficiency.

"No shit!"

And when he ran past the Blue Tent, those two people now stood beside a cauldron. They were holding hands, and their eyes were closed as if in prayer. Stanley wanted to laugh at them too, but he didn't. Instead, he just kept running until the burning in his lungs forced him to sit on a large rock.

> *…Stay in your peaceful valley, drink from the golden spring and die there…*

After another minute, Stanley stood up and walked home.

After slamming the door shut, he flipped on the light switch, stormed into the front room, fell back on the couch and swung his feet up on the coffee table.

He tried to clear his head while staring into the blank TV screen across from him. On the wall, above the TV, Thel had mounted a framed print of *Lady Gaia* by one of her favorite artists named Lynden Saint Victor. There were also two additional prints in the hallway. One was a mixed collage of suburban and cosmic images entitled *Euripides' Dream.* The other displayed the *Three Graces* from Classic Mythology. And a few inches above his head were three 8x11 sepia drawings by Thel. But they weren't just drawings. They were what Thel called Fusion Art, integrating three sepia portraitures (of themselves) into her drawings. Each drawing presented a seamless and multiple visual, depicting the couple's time in New York. The first showed them on the Lower East side of Manhattan. The second was at a cemetery and the third displayed them in Central Park. At a glance, Thel's compositions appeared three-dimensional due in part to the merging of the two mediums, enhancing Thel's technique for abstract realism. The purpose, according to

Thel, was to achieve this *Trompe l' oeil* effect. And she succeeded.

Only now Stanley had the urge to reach up and throw her drawings across the room. That's exactly what he wanted to do…and burn them.

Instead, he decided to get a drink before his impulses got the best of him. Standing by the kitchen sink, he first downed a glass of water. He next found a less than half-filled bottle of Red Wine in one of the cupboards. He popped the cork and brought the bottle to his lips. The taste was sweet and mildly bitter. After a second swig, he took the bottle with him and returned to the couch. He placed it on the coffee table and pulled out a pack of Camel non-filters from his pocket. Keeping his eyes on the blank TV screen, he lit up and took a heavy drag. Then he downed mouthful after mouthful of wine until the bottle went dry. Feeling somewhat high, he no longer cared how it all went wrong.

*

About ten minutes later he took a hot shower. After his final rinse, he turned off the water, dried himself and heard the phone ring from the kitchen. He didn't answer it. And it stopped before the answering machine had time to pick up. Thel still wasn't home.

Rummaging through the cupboard for more to drink, he found a bottle of Scotch. He took a long swallow. It squeezed his throat with a sharp pinch, but a warm comfortable glow settled in soon enough. With Scotch in tow, he went to the couch where a heaviness pressed upon his chest and seeped through his skin. Gazing at the empty wine bottle on the table, he brought the Scotch to his lips, took another long swallow and lit up another cigarette. A few minutes later, the sound of rain hit the roof like a shower of stones, loud and destructive. It had to be hail, Stanley thought. In any case, he felt the comfort in nature's maximum disorder.

What a fucking night...a most forgettable night!

Nearly an hour after Stanley came home, Thel was still out...out in the rain. Now his heart raced. Calmness slipped away, as keen-edged anxiety carved into his brain like a meat cleaver. All at once he put the scotch down, dropped the cigarette into the empty wine bottle, sprang from the couch, dashed to the bedroom, got dressed, threw on his jacket and grabbed Thel's raincoat. When he caught her scent on it, sweat ran down his face. His eyes burned as he ran to the foyer. Opening the door,

Stanley cried out in shock and dropped Thel's coat to the floor. She stood on the porch holding the picnic basket.

Drenched from head to toe, she smiled as her eyes radiated with this mystifying gleam, her face incandescent and vibrant despite being soaked from the rain. Her countenance exuded something mysterious as she stepped inside, dropped the basket, threw her arms around Stanley's neck and gave him a hard kiss on the lips. Overwhelmed by the moment, he dismissed the sense of something unfamiliar...something different...

Hereafter, she rushed past him, peeled off her blue sweater and threw it on the coffee table. She stood there a moment to catch her breath, her eyes bright with excitement. "Oh my god, Stanley! I saw the most amazing thing after you left...*the most amazing thing*! I am so...oh wow. It-it was so beautiful!"

Her hands were whizzing through the air like two hummingbirds whizzing above a bed of flowers.

"What was it?" he asked, confounded.

She looked straight up towards the ceiling with hands raised high into the air to emphasize her marvel. "Where do I begin?"

At that moment a feeling of resignation overcame Stanley when he noticed the ring removed from her finger. It had been replaced by a…band aid?

"Your finger okay?" he asked.

Thel laughed. "Oh my. Yes. My finger's fine. It's fine." And she went to the table, reached for her sweater and slid the ring out from the pocket. With a calm expression, she took a deep breath and approached Stanley. "Here," she said, placing the ring in the palm of his hand. He clasped it between forefinger and thumb as if it were now a dead spider. Seeing the slightest touch of blood on the gold band, he grimaced with threadbare melancholy. After scraping the blood off using his thumbnail, he quickly dropped the ring into his jacket pocket.

"I still love you," Thel said gently, "But I've seen something tonight that could change our lives forever."

"What?"

"Remember those two people we saw on the beach?"

It took a moment for Stanley to register her question. "You mean those weirdos with the blue tent and all those bottles?"

Thel laughed. "Well...They must be from another country. That's for sure. They had heavy accents."

"You talked to them?"

She rubbed her forehead. "Very little. But the guy gave me this band aid, because the ring tore a little skin off."

Stanley recoiled feeling all the more flustered. "I'm really sorry about that."

Thel shook her head. "Let's not worry about that now. Just close the door."

He sauntered back and closed it, slamming the deadbolt in place. "So what did you see that could change our lives forever?" But when he turned around, he froze aghast.

Thel had since peeled off her white cotton dress and undergarments. She stood completely naked and gave Stanley a sultry look and smiled. "Come on," she whispered.

*

This strange absorbing element in Thel's face burned away Stanley's melancholy like a flame-torch to a block of ice. After she helped him undress, they fell onto the bed. Thel wasted no time kissing Stanley's neck and moving on top of him, her hands hungrily caressing his chest. And as she brought her lips to his, they both closed their eyes. It was a kiss heated by heavy breathing…It was a kiss that took them somewhere far away. Thel soon grasped onto Stanley, already excitably hardened. When she guided him into her, he felt a hot wetness tightly squeeze around his swollen lingam. He gasped as did she. Both their eyes now opened and glazed over in ecstasy. Moments later a wonderful throbbing pulled them together with Thel tilting her head, licking her lips and rolling her eyes back. And when her mouth opened, she cried out.

At an instant an uncontrollable spasm took hold of their bodies. They shuddered simultaneously, sweat dripping down their skin like boiling oil. Once they found their rhythm, Thel leveled her head and looked directly into Stanley's eyes.

"The storm's relentless," she moaned, her voice heavy with a husky timbre.

"Unbelievable… "

She laughed orgasmically. "I love it!"

"Is this really happening?"

"Does it frighten you?"

"Yes."

"It's a storm, Stanley. Doesn't that thunder sound lovely? It's like a symphony...something by Wagner."

"I haven't… I've never been in the middle of a storm like this. It's like being…"

"What?"

"…In the eye of the storm."

Thel leaned back with a facetious expression on her face. The strangeness in her eyes darkened as she moved faster. And Stanley weakened, wanting to let go.

"It feels so good," Thel panted.

Her face looked dreamy and hypnotic. She cried out again. And her body moved with increased intensity, her violent thrusting in complete control. Stanley now felt as if he had crossed a threshold from which there was no return. And when Thel leaned down to press her lips against his, she shoved her tongue deep into his mouth. Bewildered, he abruptly released and came hard deep within her…

Thel lifted her head. "Oh god," she moaned. "I can feel it."

*

Thel slid off and lay next to him. They were both covered in sweat and each breathed heavily. Stanley felt both exhausted and exhilarated, a subtle buzz swimming through his every bone. For the next five minutes or so they held hands quietly until Thel groaned. "I am so hungry." And her stomach growled audibly. "See?"

He laughed and patted her belly gently.

"How about you make me your famous scrambled eggs," she said.

Stanley slid up on one elbow. "Wait a minute. What the hell happened to you out there anyway? I've never seen you like this."

She smiled and combed his hair with her fingers. "I'll tell you all about it after we eat, ok? Now please! I'm dying for those delicious eggs, huh?"

"You mean the ones with red chili?"

"Yeah!" she exclaimed, snapping her fingers. "And I'm gonna take a quick shower." She jumped out of bed, pranced to the bathroom and closed the door. Several minutes later Stanley crawled out of bed and went to the spare bathroom to clean up. After that he returned to the bedroom, threw on his pants and made his way towards the kitchen. That's when he noticed the picnic basket still in the foyer where Thel had left it. Picking up the brown willow hamper, he felt the weight of the wine bottle rolling around inside. He smiled thinking ahead about opening it for their late-night repast. And he became relieved by the thought of how this night would end on a fine note, when all that happened earlier might be forgotten. However, a quaint object, sticking out from Thel's sweater pocket, caught his attention. It looked like a small glass bottle...about a half ounce size similar to what *that strange girl* had at the beach. After placing the basket on the kitchen counter, he hurried back to the coffee table and discovered the bottle to also be filled with…

…blood? That's what it looked like anyway...

He thought.

He pulled the bottle out from her sweater pocket, unscrewed the cap and sniffed its contents. His nose twitched expecting that pungent, coppery smell of blood to shoot up from the bottle. But no. That's not what happened. Instead, a sweet, pleasant smell happily danced its way up his nostrils. And it smelled just like…*Licorice?* That's what he ultimately concluded.

How strange, he thought. It smelled really good. By no means did it have that coppery-sweetness like blood. No. It definitely did not.

He wanted to take another sniff but a funny feeling shifted deep within his head, followed by a sharp dizziness.

"Jesus!" he gasped, almost taking a spill before the dizziness soon abated. Nevertheless, his brain was now soaked in a warm fuzziness, where nothing around him felt real, as if he had been extricated from the entanglements of the world. Consequently a big smile stretched across his face, while laughter began to bubble up his throat. But movement in the hallway quickly curtailed any potentialities for hysterical laughter. Quickly, he screwed the cap back on and dropped the bottle back into the sweater pocket. He rushed back into the kitchen still feeling strangely delirious. And the smile refused to surrender. For some reason he pictured himself in a small bubble floating up into the sky. And once it popped, he'd pop right along with it. That's how he felt. Yet he somehow managed to collect his faculties and all the necessities for a good dinner. And as he began to slice 'n dice the onions, Thel walked into the kitchen freshly showered and clad in a green bathrobe. She went straight for the picnic basket, pulled out the wine, grabbed a corkscrew and opened the bottle. She filled up two wine glasses and gave one to Stanley. They tapped their rims and drank to a wordless cheer. After that she opened the fridge. "We still have some of that papya?"

"I think so," he said.

"Ah-ha!" she exclaimed excitedly. "We do."

And so Thel sliced the fruit while Stanley now sliced the tomatos. During the silence, the delirium clittered across his brain like a beetle.

If not blood, then what was it? He thought. *And what was Thel doing with that bottle anyway?*

He wanted to ask her about it but didn't want to spoil the afterglow of *making love*, especially if she knew he had been snooping through her sweater. He just hoped she intended to explain everything to him.

Once Thel finished with the papya, she found some leftover ham in the fridge and threw it into a pan. Meanwhile he threw about five eggs into a bowl along with salt, pepper and lots of red chili. The ham sizzled while he scrambled the eggs.

"Ah, it smells so good," she said, turning the ham over until it was hot. Next she placed it on a paper plate to cut it down the middle. After that, she dropped two pieces of bread into the toaster. As Stanley poured the eggs into the pan they simmered loudly. Next he stirred in the onions, tomatoes and cheese. That's when Thel stepped behind him, slid her arms around his waist and rested her head on his shoulder.

"You're probably wondering about that bottle in my sweater," she whispered into his ear.

Stanley jumped with a start, and his hand almost slipped into the simmering eggs. She stepped back laughing.

"How did you...?" he gasped, turning towards her. She had this self assured look on her face.

Maybe she did see me snoop through her sweater after all.

He thought.

The hairs from the back of his neck stiffened.

Thel waved him off good-naturedly. "I'll tell you all about it after we eat."

Stanley turned the heat down once the eggs were about done. And when he thought of Thel being left at the beach and in the rain, shame hit him hard like a blow to the gut. He cringed and covered his face with both hands.

"What's wrong?" she asked, pushing his hands aside.

"Never again," he whispered. "Never again."

"What is it?"

"I'm so sorry."

"For what?"

"Leaving you at the beach."

For the first time since coming home, Thel fell into a meditative state. Soundless words marched across her eyes, and it gave Stanley a chill. He found it bizarre. Unlike never before, did she now possess this unrecognizable aura within her. He sensed it but couldn't pinpoint exactly what it was or how to describe it. Whether or not it had anything to do with those strange people momentarily hung in the balance. Whatever the cause, it definitively affected her in some unfamiliar way…insofar as this indrawn mystery manifesting within her.

Now with a thoughtful look, she slowly nodded her head, her face collapsing into a rueful expression. When the toast popped up, she stepped forward and gripped Stanley's face with her right hand. "I hated you then," she said demonstratively. "And I'm sure you hated me too. But what does it matter now? Here we are." And she pressed her lips against his.

His eyes closed as he embraced her; she radiating with lavender. There also were the aromas of honeysuckle enriching her hair. He held her close knowing this to be one of those rarest of moments when time stands still, yielding to an awakening revealing a ray of light in a boundless night.

She was right. For all that mattered was the NOW...

he thought.

He no longer cared about the small bottle or anything else. And so they held each other, lost in a silence so deafening that it drowned out the storm from outside. Her hand now gently touched the right side of his face. "Let's eat."

Once everything had been brought to the kitchen table, they finally sat down. He buttered the toast, and she refilled their wine glasses.   Thel meant what she said about being hungry. After piling ham and eggs onto her toast, she attacked it all-including the mango. Her plate was licked clean in minutes. Groaning with pleasure, she then washed it down with the last of her wine.   And upon hearing how the wine went down her throat, Stanley felt a twitch between his legs. Managing only a couple bites of food, he couldn't stop staring at her.

Expelling a hearty belch, Thel gave Stanley a seductive look and smiled.   "That was delicious, my dear man.   You still have the touch."   She winked wiping her mouth with a napkin.   Right at that point a full throbbing came to life from down below Stanley's waist.   He couldn't help it. Whatever the cause of this mysterious change in Thel, he wanted her all the more. She dripped with sexuality, and the sweet torture of desire overwhelmed him completely.   It's possible that small bottle contained nothing more than a very potent aphrodisiac.

She laughed. "What's the matter, Stanley?"

"Huh?"

"What's with that funny smile on your face? And why aren't you eating?"

He cleared his throat, embarrassed.   "To be honest, I'm still a little ah...well..."

At first she looked puzzled, but soon her own funny smile crept across her face. She reached over and slowly slid her hand up between his thighs. "Oh! Is that for me?"

This desire had no limits, and the pain was staggering for him.

They went back into the bedroom and undressed. He eagerly slid under the covers while she stood naked beside the bed tying her hair back. Her soft round breasts half floated along with her every movement. And when she lifted her arms to stretch, her body swelled like the smoothness of a morning wave. And burning arrows of desire pierced Stanley's flesh. Before long she slid into bed and wrapped her leg around his, her toes tickling his ankle. His nose drank in her floral sweetness of lavender and honeysuckle. All of a sudden she pulled on his chest hairs hard enough to make him yelp. She laughed. Fully aroused, he began to caress her belly. Her flesh was smooth like Persian silk, and her inner thighs were feverish. Soon they moved beneath the covers like currents beneath the Chilean seas. He tried to mount her, but she pushed him back, reached under the sheet and clasped onto his lingam. He lost his breath and melted into the bed feeling her squeeze and caress him with slow long strokes.

"I want to suck your cock," she whispered, before slipping under the sheets. The warm, wet sensation of her mouth slowly slid down over him. She began to gently suck while wrapping her fingers around the base and stroking him slowly...squeezing. She took more of it in, pushing down, pulling up and moving faster and faster. It was relentless, the way she squeezed and caressed his orbs. He felt the pressure building. She had him entirely at her mercy...and he recalled how the sound of the wine poured down her throat...He could no longer control it. With sudden force, it all streamed out, the explosion painfully euphoric, sucking him inside out. And Thel swallowed it all!

Ensuingly, she slid out from under the sheets and went to the bathroom. He remained paralyzed in bed. Once she came back, she lay close to him and took his hand.

"Better?"

"My god" he said, breathlessly.

They continued to lie there falling into a quiet contemplation. He felt extremely relaxed. And soon he saw strange images of natural objects slowly appear on the ceiling from up above...

Rivers...Trees...Grass...Rocks...mountains...brown horses...crystal buildings...stars...terra cotta faces...parasols...a strawberry mist ...teardrops...the Creeping Jenny...a graveyard...

Stanley found something pleasant yet sorrowful about all those images. He wondered if they were all a projection of a dream to come, signaling his readiness to fall asleep; ready to play a part of some fantastical journey. But soon he remembered…Thel had once described those very same images to him when they first met…How strange that it all spontaneously came to mind. And the vividness of it? He rapidly became very sleepy.

"Hey. Don't you want to know what happened?" Thel asked, shaking him awake.

He sat up and slapped both sides of his face chasing away the drowsiness and those empyrean images. "Yes! Of course."

She gave him a baffled look and chortled. "Silly man. Here." She lit a cigarette and gave it to him.

"So you ready?"

"I'm all ears," he said, exhaling a bluish smoke through his nose.

With apparent fascination, Thel studied the way the smoke swirled up into the air dissolving into nothing. Her lips twitched before she spoke. "Now when I finally pulled the ring off, I hated you so much…"

CHAPTER 20

"Thanks for reminding me," Stanley groaned.

She laughed and slapped his arm. "I don't hate you now. Just let me finish, will you? Walking along the shoreline, I had every intent to throw the ring into the water. Yes, I really hated you at the time. But right when I was about to hurl the ring away for good, a powerful smell caught my attention. It smelled sweet like…hmm. I don't know…like…like being at a carnival."

"Like licorice?" he suggested.

Thel's eyes brightened. "Yes! Come to think of it. That's exactly how it smelled." The look in her eyes deepened, her eyes probing his face. "Nicely done, Stanley."

He almost said something about opening the small bottle but thought better of it. Instead, he took one last drag from his smoke and stubbed it out in a plastic cup on the nightstand.

"Anyway," she continued, "it smelled so good. I soon realized it came from that fire pit belonging to those people. Sure enough, I saw that girl pouring something from one of the little bottles into this small pot. When she saw me, I almost ran. But she smiled, her eyes glimmering kindly. She waved for me to come closer.

'"I am Trina,"' she said in a very soft, heavily accented voice. Maybe Russian. I'm not sure.

'I too introduced myself.

'Then she pointed to the man coming out of the blue tent. '"He is Pieter."'

'I waved, but he didn't smile or wave back. He grunted and went back into the tent. I was taken aback and wondered what I did wrong. Troubled, I shot a glance towards Trina, but she was busy packing some of her empty bottles into a large teardrop bag.

'"It is beautiful night, yes?"'

'"Very beautiful,"' I said. '"M-may I ask what you guys are doing?"'

'Trina smiled. '"You stay and watch, ok?"'

'But I became apprehensive by how Pieter reacted towards me. I don't think he wanted me around. During all that time he'd been rustling through the tent as if looking for something. And before you know it, out of nowhere he was towering right over me. I almost screamed. I didn't even hear him walk up to me. That was so weird. He had to have been at least seven feet. Also, I couldn't help but notice this amazing tattoo on his bare chest. The image was grotesque yet beautiful, reminding me of gothic art. At last, I realized it to be the artwork of Gustave Dore! I couldn't believe it!"

Stanley interrupted Thel with a question about who he was.

And so she explained to him Dore's grand visual interpretation of Dante's *Divine Comedy* and how pleased Stanley would be to see justice given to Dore's depiction of Charon on this guy's torso.

"And I told him how wonderful his tattoo was," Thel continued. "Of course I bombarded him with all kinds of questions about his affinity with the art and what it meant to him. But all he did was smile…finally, and he handed me a band aid.

'"For your finger, ok?"' he said, pointing towards my hand.

'I laughed nervously and took the band aid from him. '"Thank you."'

'He nodded. '"You like to stay and see a nice thing, eh?"'

'I shrugged, feeling more at ease.

'Without saying anything else, he easily took one enormous step towards Trina.

'They now stood on the other side of the fire pit. She elevated another small bottle high above the pot. They gazed upon this one bottle with reverence before closing their eyes. I'm not sure if they were praying or what. But they were definitely chanting in some other language. I obviously stumbled upon some kind of ritual. Wondering if they were trying to get me to join in their ceremony, I decided to get the hell out of there…But I noticed the strangest thing."

"What?"

"The liquid in the bottle began to change colors. It was unbelievable! I couldn't look away. The red color turned Gold, followed by crystal clear water, turning Silver, turning back to its original crimson color and so on repeating the cycle over again."

"Really?"

"Not only that but get this. When Trina finally poured the contents of this bottle into the pot, smoke shot up into the sky like an explosion! It formed this little mushroom cloud, hovering above the pot. And it remained perfectly still! It didn't move, Stanley. The cloud remained perfectly still. It was fucking incredible.

'And right at that moment, I began to feel funny and had to sit down. It was the strangest sensation like getting high but different somehow. Despite the warm and seductive buzzing in my head, I remained cogent and keenly aware of all that happened and still remember it as if it happened only seconds ago…not like ageless dreams, paranoia or a drug induced stupor. It was more like being at the center of a spinning wheel…neither moving nor completely still. It was timeless.   And that's when beautiful, gorgeous images came together in that one strange cloud. At first I thought it was just an optical illusion, but it all became so vivid, so colorful, so captivating. I couldn't look away. It came to life like a vision in 3D. And I now was within this vision. Without questioning *the how*, I just accepted being a part of it, walking among those images. Like a dream, time or space held no relevance, no transition or sequencing, yet it preserved a clear understanding of what it all meant. I never before experienced anything like this. And when it was over, I found myself crying my eyes out; not from sadness but from the sheer joy of this astonishing experience. It was like an awakening. I couldn't stop crying."

"So what did you see?"

Thel winked. "Oh you'll have to wait, Stanley. You'll just have to wait. It must be a surprise. And you will be amazed."

"A surprise? What do you mean by that?"

"All in good time, Stanley. All in good time."

Nonplussed, he tilted his head. *"All in good time?"*

Her eyes narrowed gleefully as a mischievous smirk crept across her face. "All in good time, Stanley."

He growled, exasperated. "You're killing me!"

"Haha!" she responded, lifting her hands up triumphantly. And she jumped out of bed, ran out of the room and returned with the small bottle in hand. She sat across from Stanley and began to examine it. Now the time had come to finally gather a full rounded understanding of a peculiar object filled with a peculiar potion. This brought about some indemnity for Stanley, since he had to wait *all in good time* for her so-called surprise.

"So what do you think's in that bottle?" he asked.

"I don't know," she said plainly. "I don't know."

"Has it changed colors?"

"No."

"Have you smelled it?"

She shot him a sharp glance. "Not yet."

He looked down and cleared his throat. "Well how did you get it? Did those people just give it to you?"

Thel rubbed her chin. "Again…I don't know."

"You don't know?"

"You see. This is where it gets really strange. They disappeared."

"*What?*"

Thel took a deep breath, her face shifting to a cogitative stupor. "Yeah. When the vision was over I was just sitting there alone. It was quite the mystery. Those people were gone. The tent was gone. Everything was gone except the firewood, thrown into the sand and still burning, giving off that licorice smell."

"But they were gone?"

Thel slowly nodded. "Yeah. Weird huh? I must've passed out."

"For how long?"

"Oh I don't know."

"It couldn't have been that long. I'd say you got home forty five or so minutes after me."

A wrinkle deepened between Thel's eyes, as she slowly raised the bottle above her head. "All I know is that this little bottle was next to me when I finally came to my senses. Who knows? Maybe they simply mis-placed it."

She shook the bottle but nothing changed except for little red bubbles forming at the surface. Eventually she lowered her arm. "And I just started crying. I couldn't stop. I don't know, Stanley. I don't know if…All I know is that…" She frowned and shook her head. "…once it began to rain I couldn't leave without the bottle."

She then placed it on the nightstand before stretching out next to Stanley. She crossed her hands behind her head and gazed up at the ceiling. "I don't think I'll ever see the world the same way again."

He mulled that over not precisely sure what she meant by that.

"You know what Richard Wagner once said about the Buddhist theory of the beginning of the world?"

"No."

"A breath disturbs heaven's clarity…"

"Who's Wagner by the way?"

Thel shot him a bemused look. "Only the greatest composer whoever lived. You surprise me, Stanley. The man was all about mythology. Flight of the Valkyeries? My ringtone?"

"Oh yeah. Didn't know that was him."

Thel heaved a sigh. "Whatever the case may be, I saw true magic tonight. But I'm not expecting you to believe any of what I told you. And you know that."

But he did believe her. He believed every word she said, because the change in her was evident. And that could not be denied. Nevertheless, she didn't tell him everything. Whatever she saw in that cloud, whatever she saw seemed to transport her to a place beyond his reach.

Who were those people? He thought. *What were they really? Were they part of some cult? Were they pagans? Devil worshippers? Mystics? Witches? The Mentally in-firmed? Junkies? Frauds?*

For to consider what was really in that small bottle scared him.

Stanley cleared his throat. "So did you…? Did those people…?"

Thel gave him a curious look. "What?"

He took in a deep breath not really knowing what he wanted to ask. "Did anything else happen between you and *them* that you forgot to mention?"

"Like what, Stanley?"

He shrugged with a vestige of embarrassment. "Come on, Thel. You don't know who these people were. I mean they could've-…"

She laughed. "You needn't worry, Stanley. They didn't take anything from me or ask for money. Didn't you notice I brought back the picnic basket? No. They didn't harm me in any way."

He still felt weary. "So you're okay?"

She turned away from him. "I am definitely okay."

"And you didn't ingest-…"

"No Stanley. I didn't ingest *anything*. They didn't offer me anything except a band aid and possibly that small bottle of *something*."

"Do me one favor at least."

"What?"

"Throw that bottle out." He spoke in a voice sounding more urgent than he intended.

A look of surprise and disappointment drifted across Thel's face. "Why?"

"I have a bad feeling about it," he said, struggling with a frantic buzzing in his chest.

Her face softened, accentuating the wholeness of her plain beauty. "Do you really want me to throw it out? I will if you want me to."

Transfixed by her expression, he felt an emotional shift and noticed how her eyes fulgurated strangely, like a camera flash. The frantic buzzing in his chest now quite simply…vanished.

He stammered. "D-Do what you feel's right."

"I don't know. I want to make you happy."

To Stanley, her voice poured out like a river filled with slow moving currents. And haziness languidly blew over him like a warm breeze. Again those strange images of natural objects appeared before his eyes.

Rivers…Trees…Grass…Rocks…mountains…brown horses…crystal buildings…stars…terra cotta faces…parasols…a strawberry mist…teardrops…the Creeping Jenny…a graveyard…

"You do," he responded, losing himself to an odd gleaming contentment.

"You are right about one thing, Stanley. I know nothing about those people except what I told you. And I told you everything."

"Except what you saw in the cloud."

"True. But like I said…"

"Yeah I know. All in good time."

"But let me tell you why. It's something I want to show you. I need to present it the way I saw it."

All of a sudden he was struck by a flash of intelligence. "A painting! You're going to paint what you saw in that cloud!"

Thel slowly nodded her head. "That's right, Stanley. You got it. Not only that but it's the one painting I've been trying to create all this time, the one that's been eluding me, tormenting me, the one I started the first time we met. Now I see it in full form. It'll be my magnum opus."

"The city?" he asked.

She smiled. "Yes. The city. The permanence of nature. The grandeur of human desire."

He now slid his fingers through her hair. "That's wonderful, Thel. Wonderful."

She glanced at the clock on the nightstand. "Wow. It's already two in the morning."

He yawned. "Yeah. We should get some sleep."

"I don't think so. It's time to get to work."

"On what?"

"The painting."

"*Right now*?"

"Right now." Her voice echoed vacantly.

"What's the rush?" he asked, overstepping another combative yawn. "Don't you think you should sleep first? Get a fresh start tomorrow?"

"It is tomorrow," she countered and leapt out of bed.

She ran into the closet and returned wearing her paint-stained hoodie and cargo pants; the same set of clothes she wore when Stanley first met her.

Thel now stood at the foot of the bed. "The vision is still very clear in my mind. I don't want to risk losing it if I fall asleep. Remember what I said about the clarity of heaven? Besides, I can still feel that electrical surge in my bones. It's exhilarating!"

"It's because of the wonderful sex we just had," Stanley said with a wink.

She jumped on top of him and kissed his face. "Haha! Touche my love. Touche. Now sleep. Sleep like the innocent. Sleep with a sound mind."

He heard a clangoring of…a sense of something urgent. What was it? He forgot.

Thel brought her index finger to his lips. "Now close your eyes and sleep."

CHAPTER 21

Stanley sat up, stretched and yawned. The clock on the nightstand showed 11:10am. It was Sunday morning, and a stream of sunshine poured through the bedroom window. He wondered if Thel might want to take a stroll to Quinlan's for breakfast. He awoke extremely hungry. But when he turned to wake her, her side of the bed was still empty. His first thought told him she'd be found in the basement still working on her painting. He was about to check up on her when a colorful brightness caught the corner of his eye. It came from the foot of the bed. Turning towards it, he saw…a *painting?*

Impossible! He thought.

But there it was perfectly centered on an easel. Now wide awake, he threw off the sheets. "Could it be…? Is that…? It's…My god! It's…you…It's…It's…beautiful!"

Of course his eyes were instantly drawn to the central figure of the painting…Thel's self-portrait in a blue sweater and white cotton dress, the very same clothes she wore the night before. In the painting, she looked quite real and alive standing in a lifeguard tower…*their lifeguard tower.* And beyond it stood a multi-dimensional city, filled with many strange buildings, each constructed of crystal, standing proud and mighty, all built straight up with sharp edges and massive strength.

One tower reached the stars, penetrating a beautiful constellation.

Each image was painted in such detail, ready to spring off the canvass, about 41" in width and 32" in length. There was a strawberry colored mist that crowned the building peeks and drifted downwards blanketing the streets, filled with a sundry of people: large and small, thin and fat, old and young, women and children, well-built fellows and ladies with fine-shapely legs. Some had terra cotta faces. Others looked at ease, always smiling. Women twirled gossamer-like parasols. Men twirled polished wooden canes and smoked pipes or cigars. They were all sketched in such fine insouciant detail.

There were bicycles and horse drawn carriages...A marketplace-shaped into a massive cornucopia-was filled with melons, honey, seasoned poultry, flour, sweet marjoram, fresh water, bananas, plums, berries, candied fruit, wine, beer, tobacco leaves and vegetables. And Stanley actually thought the faint scent of licorice wafted through his nose. But it lasted for only a brief moment.

...In the foreground of the tower was a garden, filled with many trees and a variety of flowers, like the bursting pinkish blooms of Azaleas and Rhododendrons, the yellow springy legion of Chrysanthemums and lastly the Creeping Jenny with coin-shaped leaves, bright and green.

"*Observe the garden*," a tiny voice fluttered up out of nowhere.

He pulled his eyes away from the painting. "Thel?" Although distant, it sounded like her voice.

Ah, smell the sweet heavenly air. Can you smell it? It's like licorice. So what do you think, Stanley? Do you like it? Look at the garden. See how the birds sing fiercely without fear...

"Where are you?" he called, jumping off the bed to look for her. "You sound so distant."

Warm currents of air constantly flow through the city. It's a serene, comforting warmth with enough strength to keep fear from crashing in...

And he finally realized her voice came from the direction of...the painting?

Slowly, he turned towards Thel's self-portrait. Then he froze unable to breath...

Her chest rose and fell in subtle rhythms. Her tiny eyes blinked as they gazed at him. Her skin glistened in rosy colors, her hair softly drifted in the air… My god!

She was alive!

No. It had to be an optical illusion. And he slowly reached out to touch the image.

"*Don't touch my face!*" she cried, holding her hands up. "*The paint's still wet!*"

Thunderstruck, he fell back onto the bed.

"Preposterous!" he laughed and cried at the same time.

Thel had painted herself into her own work of art?

"It's a dream. I'm still sleeping."

She smiled, gesturing towards the city and continued to speak in that tiny voice…almost to a whisper.

The warm breeze protects us from the razor sharp coldness of fear. It's our own paradise, leagues away from the savage heart.

Now the most important part of this painting is the garden. Pay close attention Stanley. It's eternal. Understand? Supreme and luminous.

In this place, love is alive, like the burning passion of those flowers bursting with optical colored shapes-wonderful pomegranate hues, sunflower gold, syrupy red petals, and towering oak trees, filled

yet again with more thrushes singing their euphonic melodies.

And we live in quiet solitude in our peaceful hermitage. We live

the way we want…and that's all there is.

Yes, it's so beautiful with flowers so colorful and other

brilliant foliage so robust. An upheaval of rocks breech the surface of

a renewed greenery of the ever-shifting blades of grass, reminiscent of

the dolphins we saw breech the surface of the water the other evening.

This place may seem familiar to you…?

He slowly shook his head giving in to the absurdity of

this conversation. "Not really. No."

She smiled. *"No?*

It's just a dream!

"Again look at the garden and only the garden. Ignore the rest

of the scenes. Think Stanley! It represents something else…You must

remember, right?"

"I don't..."

"You don't remember when I brought you to New York to meet my

father?

Forthwith he remembered…and he shuddered with a

terrible force! Now he realized what she meant by the

garden representing something else...

eternal. *Understand?* *Supreme and luminous*

She meant a graveyard…

Yes. A memory of the past brought him back to a time when they visited her father's gravesite. There, he sat beside Thel in front of the gravestone. It had only one inscription, a quote by William Blake…

> *Joy & Woe are woven fine;*
> *A clothing for the soul divine…*
> *Blake*

That was it. There was no name, no date of birth or when he died on 9/11.

"He once told me that's how he wanted it," she said.

After placing lotus flowers—her father's favorite—into the pot-hole, she closed her eyes and for the next few minutes remained quiet, falling into a silent meditation.

Stanley may have found the principles of faith absurd, but there was nothing absurd about this one moment. Thel held her hands close to her chest and meditated with such soulful tenderness, he almost wept. Now they were linked, each by their own tragic past. Both her father and his were ripped away from them by the savagery of humanity.

But she unexpectedly burst out laughing and threw her arms around his neck.

"Oh I love you, Stanley Reader!"

He was mystified by the unpredictable shift in her mood. Furthermore, they had only been together for a month. Until then neither of them had mentioned anything about love.

Now her eyes filled with a refulgency quite spellbinding, her smile deepening. "Don't be too concerned. Oh you must think I'm crazy. But that's okay. You don't have to say anything."

He held her hand. "It's okay. You're not that crazy."

She laughed and kissed him. Too overwhelmed to frame into words what was happening, he felt a sense of dubious wonder rise to the surface. But the longer they kissed, it was all quickly put to rest-yielding to an abrupt passion. And he did love Thel! He loved her too. Already he had long since fallen completely and hopelessly in love with her.

Again, he heard the whispering of that tiny voice bring him back to the present moment, to the presence of the painting...

"Now do you remember?"

He sadly gazed at the little figure in the lifeguard tower. "Yes."

"Good, Stan," she said with gravitas. *"But here it's a garden, thriving with life. It all just flows and flows. And do you remember what we did after I took you to see my father?"*

"We took a carriage ride through Central Park…"

"And remember how happy we were?"

"I remember...We were very happy."

Thel clapped her hands excitedly. *"What a perfect moment it was to ride through Central park with you."*

He remembered it clearly; the horse drawn carriage rolling upon the cobble streets through the park. How they sat close together, riding along during a summer evening. Holding each other, he felt so assured that their destiny was a good one. Yes. They held each other tightly, hearing the clattering of the horse's trot. He wished that moment would never end. They were together in the midst of a place filled with the greenery of trees and rolling knolls of shimmering grass.

Thel's haunting voice echoed from the canvass. "Stanley?"

"Yes?"

"There's so much more to see." And her small hand reached out to him.

Hesitating, he took a deep breath and saw the white lotus flowers blossoming in her eyes.

"Hurry Stanley before the paint dries. Otherwise it's too late. Take my hand. This is *OUR* destiny." She reached out for him. "Take my hand before it's too late."

Right at that moment Stanley's cell phone rang from in the kitchen. He looked away from the painting...from her.

"Don't answer it," she said.

His eyes fell back upon the painting. Now her charm and wonder became ambiguous. She began to fade with diminishing colors. The painting was beginning to dry.

"I'm sorry," he said, frightened by his own expectations: half mad, half doubtful.

"It's not a dream, Stan," she remonstrated. *"Take my hand before it's too late!"*

But he couldn't help but yield to a more accessible reality, where there existed the possibility the *true Thel* was calling him on the phone. And that is what forced him from the bedroom to the kitchen.

He picked up. "Hello? Thel? Where are you?"

No answer.

"Thel?"

A frequency of low static and emptiness.

"Hello!"

Now subtle breathing.

"Who is this?" he demanded.

A male's voice from the other end finally responded. "H-hi. Stan?"

"Yeah?"

"It's Matt."

Stanley clenched his jaw and cursed himself. *Goddamn you.*

His grip loosened from the phone. "Hey."

Matt cleared his throat. "Just letting you know we'll be at Tinker's tonight gettin shitfaced to kick off another grueling semester. Wanna join? Some beers, some shots, some pool. More beer, more shots. You know. Your typical Monday night blow out."

"*Monday night*? So you mean *tomorrow* night, right?"

A pause. "No," Matt said slowly. "I mean tonight. Sorry to break it to you bro but it's Monday. Haha. Hope you didn't miss your first day of class."

Stanley's throat tightened. *"What?"*

"You alright?"

Holding the phone against his ear, he ran into the living room and drew the blinds away from the window. He held his breath and stood there in absolute shock gawking at the unexpected darkness.

"Stan?"

Could I really have been staring at Thel's painting for two days and a night, losing track of that much time? Impossible. It seemed like only ten minutes. Fifteen tops.

"Hey Stan. You okay?"

He dropped the phone, took a deep breath and for the first time noticed how dark the house was. The only light came from the bedroom. And he had no recollection of ever switching on the lamp. Though to be certain the painting wasn't a figment of his imagination, he did run back into the bedroom.

"It's not a dream...Take my hand before it's too late!"

Sure enough, it was still there.

He slowly approached it from behind keeping one arm out in front of him.

Ridiculous! It's not as if this thing were alive, right? No. Of course not. But it was alive. *SHE was alive!*

He froze unable to take another step. He couldn't bring himself to face the painting again. There definitely was something unappealing about it, emitting a palpable

284

presence. It's like the bedroom or the entire house was haunted by a ghost. That's how it felt.

But I don't believe in ghosts!

In haste, he slid on his pants, sprang out of the bedroom, hurried down the basement steps and knocked on the door. Rarely did he go in. Thel kept it locked when not working. And he stayed out when she was working. This became protocol. The basement was her creative chamber, hermetically sealed off from the rest of the world. So he respected her need to be alone during what she termed self-consciously as "the stage by stage development of form." Although, she preferred to keep her work hidden until complete, she wasn't totally secretive about it. If she were stuck or lost on what she called "the sensory of color," she'd call him down for feedback. And those were the only times he stepped foot inside her makeshift art studio. He knocked again but still no answer. When he finally pushed down on the handle, the door opened.

CHAPTER 22

His nose caught the sharp smell of turpentine and linseed oil. After flipping on the lightswitch, he saw that all her equipment remained in complete and normal disarray. Palette knives, paint knives and brushes were scattered upon her work table. Towels, soaked in paint, were on the floor. Her Palette lay upon waxpaper. Nothing out of the ordinary. The place was business as usual. He called out Thel's name. With no response, he rushed back up the stairs.

First, he ran into the living room to see if her sweater was still on the table. *Gone!* Her white cotton dress was also missing, no longer on the living room floor. Next, he grabbed his cell phone from the floor. Matt's call had since been disconnected. Stanley called Thel's cell phone and hoped to hell it wouldn't go to voicemail. He waited. It began to ring. "Come on. Answer!"

But as it continued to ring, he soon heard Wagner's *Flight of the Valkeries* playing somewhere in the house. He knew right away it was her ringtone, which meant she left her phone here. And it came from the bedroom!

"You gotta be fucking kidding," he whispered.

Purposely averting his eyes from the painting, he ran back into the bedroom following the sound of the ringtone, leading him into their walk-in closet. When the ringing stopped, he called it again. And again her phone responded with Wagner's score. He turned on the closet light and heard the phone come from her cargo pants left on the floor. Her hoodie was also on the floor, the last set of clothes he remembered seeing her wear. He reached into one of the cargo pockets for her phone and saw his own number displayed.

"Unbelievable," he whispered, tossing the phone onto her pants. Not knowing her security code, he had no access to her recent calls or messages.

All her clothes were still there, including another set of work clothes: A pair of old jeans and a T-shirt saying *I believe in peace, bitch!* There they hung in all their permanent paint-stained glory.

"I don't get it," he whispered. "Where the hell are you?" Next he went into the bathroom and flipped on the light to see if by chance any of her toiletries were missing. But everything seemed to be in place. Her toothbrush was still on the sink. Her deodorant remained untouched in the medicine cabinet and her tampons were in the cupboard below the sink.

Next he searched for her purse. He figured she couldn't get very far without it. Only he had no idea where she stashed it. She rarely left her purse out in plain sight. All he could do was scour the house from top to bottom, flipping on all the lights, rifling through drawers, cupboards, searching the spare bathroom, kitchen, basement, closet and lastly the bedroom. He even checked in between the mattress for a wallet. Nothing.

"But why?" he murmured. He did find her yellow bag under the bed. But no purse, just a sketchbook and a couple charcoal pencils stashed away in her bag. Thel's flip-flops were also under the bed. That's it. Getting up from his knees, he had mixed feelings of both humiliation and trepidation. Not finding her purse meant she either placed it somewhere impossible to find or…He really didn't know what else to think; not after she returned home.

"We did patch things up, right?" he asked aloud. "It had to mean something to her. It had to…I don't understand. To leave everything behind? Your art equipment and your…your…" Strangely, Stanley couldn't bring himself to say it…He tried not to consider it. Yet his eyes took on a life all their own, rotating towards the painting. He again stood face to face with it. It looked dry alright as did the self-portrait of Thel. Her blue sweater and white cotton dress became fixed, hardened by the dried colors. Her hands now clutched the railing. Her chest had ceased to rise and fall. Her skin no longer glowed with the burning energy of life. She now became a fixity in her own masterpiece, her tiny face brightly illuminated. With great relief, he took a deep breath.

"You see?" he said to himself. "It was all part of some bad dream."

But he soon noticed something new on the canvass.

He gasped, slowly backing away and collapsing onto the bed. It felt like hell dropped into the room like a dead meteor. Below her right eye were two small crimson colored teardrops. "Those tears weren't there before," he whispered.

And her eyes kept changing colors each time he shook his head in dazed astonishment. Only when he stopped moving did they stop changing. But when he leaned closer, her eyes became colorless yet sparkled like crystal.

"This is madness!" he exclaimed.

When he leaned back, her eyes returned to those natural brown colors, glistening with the faintest signs of life.

Each time he moved, the color texture changed. From the left, her eyes gleamed with the golden radiance of the sun. From the right, her eyes shined with the silvery rays of the moon.

> *The liquid in the bottle began to change colors. It was unbelievable! I couldn't look away. The red color turned Gold, followed by crystal clear water, quickly turning Silver, turning back to its original crimson color and so on repeating the cycle over again.*

"Crimson color," he echoed, looking at those two teardrops below her right eye. Slowly he turned towards the nightstand where the small bottle had been. Gone. No bottle. No liquid.

He swallowed.

On that, his head swiveled back towards the painting. Now all he could do was stare stupidly at her eyes, the colors changing with his every move. She created her own personal myth, presenting a resurrection through postimpressionism negating the post apocalyptic. She created a tower that reached the stars...*penetrating* a beautiful constellation resembling an astronomical vulva. And when he saw the two large concentric structures, so round and circular serving as the tower's substratum he realized...yes he realized it was eternal bliss...sexual...pure and powerful! The phallic symbol within the womb of the universe. It was Thel's construct...*thee crystal Tower.*

And it was more than just a kaleidoscopic city of majestic and magical purportions. The swirling colors of gold, emerald green, glittering blue, crystal white were strong with calming tones and the images of the city were softly distorted in all its sexual and suburban splendors.

How did she do it? For any other skilled artist, it would take months, even years to complete such an elaborate assembly of beautiful enchantments both in color and structure. It didn't matter. This was her vision, the one she wanted to share...

"Is this what you meant by the peaceful valley?" he asked.

That's where we ought to be! And there's still so much more to see.

"Like what?"

And you will be amazed

"It's just a painting."

Take my hand

"Only a dream."

"It's not a dream, Stan," she remonstrated. *"Take my hand before it's too late!"*

"Before it's too late," he repeated.

As silence trailed through every crack and groove of the house, he remained seated, lost in an emptiness that felt colossal. A void spread untamed and gigantic, as darkness and daylight took turns settling on every door and wall...a cycle of hours while he continued to stare waiting...waiting for something to happen. With clenched fists, he waited for her hand to reach out to him. It never moved. He waited for those white lotus flowers to blossom in her eyes once again. They never did.

"Please Thel," he wept. "Give me another chance."

Again it had him gripped for endless hours. Eternal serenity. Prayers crushed. An irreplaceable adventure. Knowing what to believe and forgetting how to think. Judgement served in a tumbler with despair shaken and regret stirred. Cool trickles. The heart crackles. Stuck in ice. The soul cries. Both victory and defeat wrapped nicely with the joy and woe of that soul divine. How dreadful and laughable. How noble and fictional. He finally realized her painting was driving him insane. He sat there like a vague memory, beaten by fate, the unconquered savage(*And can understand nothing of it*). He didn't have the right to something this beautiful and neither did anyone else. It was enough to kill for, enough to drive anyone to absolute madness. It was too beautiful...too dangerous. And now he hated it. It was the kind of hatred strong enough to blast through a brickwall, giving him an avenue of escape. The spell had snapped somehow.

After staggering into the kitchen, he gulped down a glass of water and felt weary when mulling over how long he sat staring at that painting. He was too afraid to check the date on the clock. Instead, he returned to the bedroom to find his cell phone. It was on the carpet floor right in front of the painting. He made sure to keep his head turned away from the painting when picking up his phone. Next, he hurried out of the bedroom into the hallway where he checked his voicemail to see if Thel had called. There were 7 messages showing. He checked them all. Matt did call back and left a message asking if he was okay. His mom left a couple messages as did his employer concerned he had not shown up for work. Two instructors from University also called and each left a message inquiring about his attendance. But there was no message from Thel…Not one. Next he went to the couch to smoke a cigarette. He needed a moment to bring about a sense of reason but after a few deep pulls from his smoke, a startling thought had him off the couch.

The Ring!

He threw the cigarette into the ashtray. To hell with the painting. Where was the ring?

My jacket!

Back in the bedroom, he saw it thrown on the floor on his side of the bed. Fishing through one pocket, Stanley came up empty. A chill shot up his spine. His hand quickly dove into the other pocket and found it. He turned the ring over until noticing those expressive glittering stones.

"You see?" he said to the ring. "We made love alright! You understand me? We had dinner and shared a bottle of wine and talked throughout the night. I could still smell her on my skin. That's honeysuckle and the faint smell of lavender."

He brought the ring closer to his face and studied the sharp outlines of each stone. The illuminating sparkles of the diamond now reminded him of the crystal metropolis in Thel's painting. And the sapphires were like…like the brightly colored flowers in her optical garden. That's right. *That's right.* But he no longer wanted to think about the painting. He wanted to forget all about it, especially how Thel's small hand reached out to him.

Take my hand before it's too late…

"This is bullshit!" he cried, glaring at the stones. "It's just a lousy goddamn painting."

This is what I meant...

He shuddered and wrapped his fingers around the ring. In a knotted fist, he squeezed until the stones dug sharply into his flesh.

"Where the hell are you?" he demanded.

He thought about going to the hostel—where she used to live—to see if she returned there. She might even be at Quinlan's. What if she went back to New York? Then he considered calling Professor Miller to ask what he'd do in his place, to ask what he thought about all this, if someone had ever left him like this. He thought about all those things. Yet, he stood there for a long time unsure if that's what he really wanted to do.

You could've at least left a note, he thought, *to explain the meaning of all this.*

It finally occurred to him that her painting *was the note*. That's it! Of course. What else could it be? It was Thel's way of saying Goodbye, that it was over. There could be no other explanation for it. Her painting had to be this farewell token as a way to remember her by.

Oh, for christ's sake.

It seemed more like a symbolic gesture of plain mockery. That's all. And he wondered if when she walked out the front door, she had a smirk on her face thinking...

Too bad for you, Stanley. You could've had the real thing. But no. You just had to ask me to marry you. You just had to laugh at me. Well fuck you. And see what you get for running off the way you did? Leaving me at the beach? IN THE RAIN? Telling me to die in my own valley? Well, Fuck you Stanley Reader! Two can play at that game, eh? Adios big boy. Hope you enjoyed our last fuck. Remember it well. You'll never have it like that again. Never!

So here's a little something to remember me by...A lousy goddamn painting. Haha. Who's laughing now, big boy? Who's laughing now?

By now the sweat had dripped into his eyebrows. His whole body trembled with scorching emotions. "Fuck you too, bitch."

He turned and stomped towards the painting, grabbed it from the easel and ran it down to the basement. After dropping it-up on end-into the laundry sink, he noticed how Thel had glued the entire canvass to a mounting board. That's okay. He doubted it'd be problematic for his intent. So he went ahead checking all the top and bottom cupboards hoping to find something flammable. Sure enough, he found a one gallon metal can of boiled linseed oil. Good. It was full. First, he opened all the basement windows. Next he grabbed the metal can, unscrewed the cap and drenched the painting with the entire gallon of oil. After that he ran up the stairs for his lighter. In no time, he returned to the basement. Spinning the thumbwheel, he used all his willpower to keep his eyes away from Thel's self-portrait and to convince himself she *did not* paint herself into her own painting. That's all he could do as the flint charged a spark, the spark blossoming into a dreamy flame. Ever so slowly, it drew closer and closer to the canvass. Now he felt a tremor in his chest grow into something grotesque and magnified, beyond the realm of his own personal struggles. Burning in the hand of white heat, the dreamy flame swiftly burst into a violent blaze. Unable to now look away, he turned to see Thel's face enshrouded in a celestial circle of blinding light.

He looked into those eyes, rapidly changing colors until they peeled away from the mounting board. Black radiance voraciously consumed Thel along with the colorful wild new frontier of humanity and nature. It all vaporized into gluttonous smoke, spreading like dead tree branches across the basement and drifting out the windows. His eyes began to water, and he started coughing. Somehow, he managed to spot a rubber sink stopper stashed behind the faucet. He grabbed it, turned on the water and stuffed the plug into the drain trying not to get nipped by the flames. As the sink began to fill up, the flames began to shrink. Once the sink reached full capacity, he turned the water off. With the painting now half submerged, he splashed water over the last of the smaller flames. They quickly changed to thin streams of smoke, spreading throughout the basement. The mounting board, although warped and blistered, is all that survived, while the painting had since vaporized into nothingness.

But the smoke lingered making it difficult for Stanley to breath. When his coughing worsened, he decided to make a run for it. After closing the basement door, he tiredly climbed up the stairs while struggling to breath. Not until he got to the kitchen did the coughing finally ease up. And though he found it much easier to breath, the back of his throat felt sun baked. He drank three and a half glasses of water and wiped the sweat off his face with a paper towel. Then he leaned back against the kitchen sink, crossed his arms, bowed his head and closed his eyes.

A strange presence remained...a perfect stillness consumed by the burning smell of a peaceful valley. And a malignant thought emerged from the not so distant past...

You could stay in your peaceful valley...and die there.

When his fingers began to tremble, he decided to step outside for some fresh air. There also was a bit of the sharpness in his lungs with each breath taken.

To hell with her.

What yearning remained shattered into hundreds of contemptuous little dances. And after that, a bit of relief began spreading upon the underside of his dazzling rage. Good! That's more like it. Now he walked into the living room and stood there staring at the front door. It stared back at him like a stolid fortune teller, reluctant to reveal a future that may have already happened. For some reason that's how it felt. So what. He approached the door anyway, opened it and stepped past the threshold.

And so ends the movie...

Thel's Painting

CHAPTER 23

(BACK TO THE PRESENT)

Drenched in familiar darkness, I stood upon a familiar lifeguard tower, in a familiar place where a great many stars shined from up above. I heard the ocean's turning tide. And every part of me remembered every last detail of a forgotten past. Turning around, I gazed into an empty cabin, filled with an icy draft, muddy sand and brown puddles all smashed into one primal matter of *massa confusa*. There was no house or front porch. Only this. I had opened the front door and stepped back into this…only this.

I had been here all along...standing on the top deck of this lifeguard tower. The slight pain in my leg also brought about some perspective, purveying a clear vision of the present. Eventually, my eyes were drawn towards the dim glow of a dying fire. Embers popped into the air from the charred pieces of firewood, half buried in the sand.

"Those people," I whispered. *Those fucking people whoever they were.*

"Hey!" I cried out.

But the blue tent was gone. They were gone. It was just as Thel had said…

…When the vision was over I was alone. It was quite the mystery. Those people were gone. The tent was gone. Everything was gone except the firewood, thrown into the sand and still burning, giving off that licorice smell…

And it happened once again…the same way as before. I also had a vision. No more blank spots. No more darkness. No more being stuck at the bottom of a well. I now remembered everything. And by no means was it imaginable...Thel was not imaginable…not even the painting was imaginable. The painting…Yes the painting…Thel's miraculous masterpiece…not imaginable. And that's why I tried so hard to forget it, to leave it behind…only to be brought back to it by misguided fits of hallucinations. The painting was not imaginable...

Now here I stood remembering the night she created a work of art, a work of art I destroyed. Why Thel? Why did you do it? Why did you have to paint it? If only I had stayed with you that night. Oh you must understand. I had no choice but to destroy your painting. The regret tormented me so. Don't you see? There can be no denying you did perform a miracle that night, creating a masterpiece within hours-a painting beyond the realm of logic. And it was too much for me to take. I didn't have the intelligence for it. I called it a mockery. I called you a bitch. But I spoke like a fool, poisoned by my own stupidity. How grating and oppressive the painting turned out to be. It's true. I had to free myself from the hell you created. It all had to end somehow.

Then I glared at the dying firewood and wondered who those two people truly were. Might they be sorcerers? Conjurers? Possibly. I should've taken the book instead of the beer. I could now see Miller and myself pouring over it, trying to translate and decipher the old ways of magic. Damn them. Maybe they were to be held responsible for what happened to Thel. They gave her that small bottle after all, a bottle which contained...*something*. It'd be all too convenient to call it a drug. It was far more dangerous than all that. It had power! Could it have been a magic potion? I saw what it can do. Thel did too. And Thel got what she wanted. Is that all that mattered?

It's so difficult to know for sure. Now she was gone. Those two strangers were gone. I wanted to scream. I wanted to brace myself and let out a terrible scream, a scream that would pour out like a gust of wind and sweep over the water. But nothing happened. The scream didn't come. Instead, all that came was the silky redness of the pre-dawn, beginning to brush away the harrowing planes of night, the stars slowly becoming vague and indistinct.

The swaying...the swaying of the ladder as I carefully climbed down each step. The smell of the sweet vapors...

...still burning, giving off that sweet smell...

And I approached the burning firewood, to watch the tendrils of smoke float up to where I could inhale it deep into my lungs. Yes. I staggered towards it. And as I got closer, the sweet vapors got stronger. Ahhh. It smelled so good... It all really didn't seem of much importance now, not as I got closer to the firewood.

I could not stay away from it. This was wrong...so wrong. And I knew it with each step I took. But I could not stay away. I could not help myself. Difficult to explain ...difficult to understand...I could not help myself. The wonderful smell...so wonderful...wonderful...drawing me closer...

And...

...I began to see things...

differently...

A major shift in...

C oN c IO ʊ ɱ ᴇ S S

Id en T it Y

R E a **son**

303

Expecting to escape from the abyssal waters of sadness and regret, I experienced the exact opposite instead. There was no peace of mind. There was no quiet tempo of the heart. No. That's not what happened. Rather, walking up to the firewood was more like descending down into my own inferno.

If only I could accept the painting for all that it was…just a lousy goddamn painting. But I knew better. No one knew more than I how she struggled with it for so long, trying to piece it all together. And when Thel finally did, in completing her painting, she offered me her hand. But what I did instead was…oh my god. And Emily knew…she knew…I told her so.

I had to laugh. Haha! I really did. Hahaha! Who was I kidding? Madness did wonders to say the least, stretching one night into endless doom. Good night and adieu.

Ah Yes. This is how it should've always been...acceptance, acceptance and nothing more. And when I thought about Emily, a crooked smile pressed upon my lips. Remembering how she had leaned up against me, I felt that bitter longing once again. But why go on? When desire struck I gave in to a kiss. For that brief moment, I danced to noiseless music, flowers falling from the sky. And somewhere in the distance, a delightful laugh tumbled out like a love song. No matter.

Emily now possessed her own memory of death, served to her like poison in a tin cup. And I wondered if she'd ever want to see me again. I wanted to see her again, to make sure that what happened tonight wouldn't affect her too much. She had to survive and continue on. She had to live.

But when my eyes fell upon my own dirty hands, I was struck by my own stupidity. How could I help her if I couldn't help myself? She had no time for murderers. Call it a beast within or primal desires ripping the life out of the true beauty of the world. Call it something *monstrous*. For in the end it was always about Thel. And it could be no other way.

So what if my memories were no longer fragmented, if the truths were no longer buried with the dead, if the war played itself out with so many gruesome deaths or that by destroying Thel's painting meant…her death. Even tonight's shooting carried some relevance. All would be seared to memory forever. Apparitions or phantoms, I accepted them all as the one supreme ordeal, an ordeal like a dead rose in my breast pocket. I'd see it in the mirror. It'd be with me at the kitchen table. I'd now carry it with tranquility.

Yes. They were all too real—those Crises Apparitions. For I now believed in ghosts.

Stepping towards the water, I observed how the waves kept coming in, one after another, rising, taking on their own distinct form, some bigger than others and all diminishing, until they dissolved into the sand, into nothing. Yet they continued to come. They just kept coming, moving forward, each wave different. Nonetheless, they were all just waves, riding out the length of the tide, the cycle never stopping, encompassing both form and nothingness, reminding me of one full lifetime of man. And once again those natural objects came to mind, strange images of the…

> *Rivers…Trees…Grass…Rocks…mountains…brown horses…crystal buildings...stars…terra cotta faces…parasols…a strawberry mist…teardrops…the Creeping Jenny…a graveyard…*

Those images found their place in Thel's painting. Those images had always been with her. And they had been with me since the first time I met her. Those images created a landscape filled with the density of bliss, of a world that had to exist somewhere. And I thought about the way Thel's eyes came to life, the way they changed colors. She had fulfilled a destiny that could no longer be dismissed. That's right. The ocean may have smelled like rot, but there were many stars in the sky. And they all found their own freedom, their bodies sparkling with the fullness of life. They each danced without moving, settled upon a fixed point beyond the confinement of time. And so in the tower was where that stillness of Thel's figure once stood, fixed and dancing, as I stood here, fixed in my own solitude. The world I once knew had since been annihilated…and all was well. It's true because here, at the lifeguard tower, is where I had to be. Thel led me out of my room. And I followed her to all our sweet places, to where I now arrived here at the Western's edge, to where the world now came to an end. This was where I'd be able to step into Thel's painting once and for all.

Then I reached into my pocket for the ring. Taking it from the jewel box, I held it in my hand and looked out into the horizon. The pre-dawn morning grew warm, with an indolent breeze coming off the Pacific. And beyond the horizon, towering high above the sea was the crystal tower. Far beyond something like a natural phenomenon, Thel's immense construction radiated this blinding white blaze. To the naked eye, no outline was visible due in part to the rippling air of white heat, similar to the surface of a desert highway when the sun's at its apex. Her towering pillar glowed in all its heavenly brilliance, further

307

illumined by the ghostly stillness of the moonlight.

"It's beautiful," I said, stepping into the water. This moment had been weighed down with so heavy a silence, yet brightened by so great a spectacle indeed. With both feet submerged in water, I stood motionless overwhelmed by the grandeur of that flaring pillar. It had the very same affect on me as it did in the painting so long ago. Now I was in it, within this painting, whereupon the pillar shined more than ever. And it appeared to look more like a spectral tower.

Of course the coastal environ brimmed with the scent of *Lavender,* along with the fullest sense of the waves splashing against my knees. But as I was about to swim out to the tower…to be with Thel forever…

…*this high-pitched bellowing roar* erupted out of nowhere. It shattered the tranquility of this shadowy dawn. I looked around but saw only darkness, not quite moved by the stirrings of the new day…

Naturally, I sensed this disturbance close by, the sound ominous and terrifying. Clearly beyond my scope of comprehension, incongruous to this coastal setting, I had no idea what to make of it. Then I gasped feeling the cold biting of the sea for the first time. At the same instant, the scent of lavender vanished...so quickly did it vanish. Panicked, I looked out to sea only to discover the crystal tower had...also vanished.

"No!" I exclaimed, about to move farther out into the water. Yet subtle movements caught the left corner of my eye. I turned and saw what appeared to be a shadow in the shape of a human figure! How strange that I failed to notice this before. Whatever the case, this unknown figure stood motionless except for the severe rise and fall of the shoulders (the movements, which had probably caught my attention?). That might have been due to the breathing, occurring at rapid intervals. Apparently unaware of my presence, this shadow also stared straight ahead to where the tower had once been. It now occurred to me that it might be...

But of course! It had to be her. Who else could it be? Cautiously, I stepped out of the water and stayed focused on the shadow. Indeed, there was something familiar about the appearance, even the presence for that matter, as the shoulders continued to move in sync with the heavy breathing. I took a step closer but still could not make out the face. *"Thel?"* I said, struck with the force of exhilaration. "Is that you?"

Taking another step, I could partially see the face, though not enough to identify it with certainty. "Thel?"

The shadow suddenly released a guttural shriek.

I lunged back, my heart dropping to the bottom of my gut. No. That was not Thel. Yet the profile continued to look quite familiar, now visible from the morning reddish rays. At last I finally recognized her. "Emily!"

"Is it gone?" She asked.

"What?"

"The lion! Is it gone?"

Astounded, I cleared my throat. "Did you say *lion*?"

Emily's head jerked from side to side, her eyes wide with terror. In no time she ran towards me, her hands flailing in the air. "Yes!" she exclaimed. "There's a lion on the loose!"

Temporarily breaking away from the present, I heard

another familiar voice echo...

There's a lion on the loose...okay?

Right then Emily grabbed onto my arm. "Come on, Stanley! We need to get the hell out of here."

Her eyes darted in all directions until something caught her attention. And it struck her with a force of great relief. "Perfect!" She cried, leading me back towards *the lifeguard tower*. "Come on."

"Hey wait a minute," I said. "What the hell are you doing out here anyway?"

Emily shot me a glare. "Why do you think?"

And she picked up the pace. "But what I now can't stop thinking about is how that lion kept breathing on me, its breath hot and thick. And that huffing and sniffing sound? Oh god! Then I felt this solid mass of wetness brush across the back of my legs. At first I thought it was just a really big dog until I heard that dreadful roar. Holy fuck! You must've heard it too, right? I was scared shitless. I couldn't move. No way in hell could I move. That roar...ah...to...ah...oh god!" She shuddered but wasted no time climbing up the ladder to the tower.

"I felt those eyes penetrate right through my back," she panted. "I couldn't move! I just couldn't move. But from the corner of my eye, I caught a glimpse of it. I saw it. I saw it I tell you!"

After making it to the top, she turned around and looked down at me. "And it was a goddamn lion! And like a fool I just stood there waiting…waiting to die…then you showed up. Didn't you see it? What the hell is a lion doing on the beach, Stanley?"

"I don't know," I said, gazing out towards the water. And on the slope of each approaching wave, I saw a lion with sinewy haunches and a mountainous head, enshrouded by a thick, golden mane, his eyes filled with the sparkles of gold, silver and red, the colors changing so fast a fire seemed to ignite in each eye. And his name was Samson.

Did that lion trainer really let him go? Jesus Christ! And come to find out Emily was nearly eaten alive. Goddamn him. Goddamn that fucking maniac. But I do remember his advice about standing still when confronted by a lion. It's a good thing Emily did just that.

"Come on, Stan," she gasped. "What are you waiting for? Hurry up! That thing was here just seconds ago. It's gotta be somewhere close by."

But right when I was about to climb up the ladder, it occurred to me I no longer had the ring in my hand. Shit! I checked my pockets. Nothing. It must've dropped.

"What's wrong?"

"The ring," I said, turning around. "I dropped Thel's ring somewhere in the sand."

"Fuck the ring!" Emily cried. *"Are you nuts?* There's a goddamn lion on the loose. Get up here now!"

But I began retracing my steps checking for anything that glittered in the sand.

"Stanley you idiot!" Emily yelled. "Look at me."

I turned back and saw her take a couple steps down the ladder. "I came out here looking for you, understand? *I came out here looking for you!* Now listen very carefully. We can survive this. No need to go unhinged for a ring. Let's turn our backs on all this. And that will be the way of things. Just get your ass up here." She reached out to me. "Now take my hand before it's too late!"

At that moment it all came to a grinding halt. Even the sound of the ocean got sucked into the vast nothingness

313

of a void, while Emily's eyes filled up with a startling bright reflection from beyond the horizon of the sea...

The EnD

Raw Poetry

Two selected tales

By
Remy Kirkham

Raw Poetry

The night brought a black sky that didn't know the meaning of existence. It was like a dome sealing a flat world shut, a place that was incurable and just plain fucked up. There was no escape. And in this impervious darkness a "no vacancy" sign tiredly flashed away while the motel sign didn't flash at all. In one room a misogynistic dwarf fucked a whore's brains out. In another room, a glassy eyed marine just wanted to be left alone with his dime's worth of warm junk. And though his eyes were glued to the TV screen, he paid no attention to John Wayne playing a soldier. All other occupants slept, dreaming about unfamiliar creatures or things to be forgotten by morning.

Cars flowed down the highway like a polluted river. Beyond that, a young man in a black coat staggered out of the local bar with a purse. He was laughing hysterically. Then he waited until a dented Ford pickup swerved to the curb. He jumped in before it sped away. A few minutes later an aging poet stepped out with a grim expression on her face. She looked from one end of the block to the other end. She was looking for the young man in the black coat. She thought about going back to the bathroom just to be sure. But she knew…she knew…And only then did she realize her blouse was still unbuttoned.

"Fucking bastard," she murmured, still feeling the strength of his cock in her mouth. Slowly, she looked up into the sky, empty and careless. So she turned around and walked back into the bar to finish the last of her Negroni. All at once words of poetry suddenly surged through her heart like 2300 volts of electricity. Her whole body stiffened. The words came without warning, demanding to be written. And the poet knew why. So the poet had no choice but to ask the bartender for a pencil and slip of paper. Once the poet got started, the poet couldn't stop. The pencil took on a life all its own. The old poet's eyes shined like twin stars. And it was glorious! For the night's indifference brought to her a masterpiece indeed. Meanwhile the whore had since taken her money and fled from the misogynistic dwarf, who snored away on cold sheets. In the other room, the marine remained glassy eyed, though his eyes were no longer glued to the TV screen. And somewhere in the impervious darkness, hysterical laughter never ceased, as the "No Vacancy" sign continued to flash tiredly.

The enD

Lost in Java

My heads killing me, the worst headache in the world, my
eyes hurt. I need coffee. It's hot and I have no idea where
I am, except that it's all desert. But there's this little
coffeehouse in the midst of it all. I try to figure out
why. It doesn't matter. I go in. There's this bespectacled
little ol' man sitting at one of the tables. His hair's
greasy white and his beard's long and tangled. When he
smiles, two front teeth are missing.

You work here?

Sure do.

Coffee?

Sure. Sit a spell.

When he gets up, he's wearing faded red overalls and no
shoes, just a pair of mismatched socks… One black, one
white. I sit away from the window, away from the glare
where it's less painful. Across from me, a young woman is
reading Calvino's Invisible Cities. Ah! It hurts just to
read. She's wearing a halter-top stitched with a sanguine
butterfly. And I smell lavender. I wonder if it's her. Our
eyes meet. She smiles, I smile. Then we look away. The ol'
man returns with my coffee. He also brings a sweet roll.

No, no. Just coffee.

Try it.

It goes good with the java, eh?

Don't worry. The rolls free.

But I couldn't even pay for the coffee. It doesn't matter.
I'm desperate, besides broke. And I notice something

peculiar about his spectacles. There's this hairline crack across the left lens. He winks.

Enjoy.

Thanks.

He returns to his table and looks out the window where the sun continues to pound away at the world. The coffee is a rich black, opaque substance and thick like black tar. But it smells sweet, like either burnt chocolate or licorice. I don't know. I'm so delirious. Maybe it doesn't smell at all. But it looks pretty bad. It doesn't matter. I'm pretty desperate. And when I drink, a miracle occurs. I mean a true miracle! Not only is it the best coffee ever, that rich toasty sweetness-neither chocolate nor licorice-just this ineffable taste that...my pounding headache vanishes completely! After only the first sip that relentless sharp pressure releases like a pop, a bottle uncorked. The relief makes me smile. And I almost feel at peace...even a little sleepy. And I can't remember the last time I slept or how I even got here. I reach into my pocket just to be sure there's no money. Nope. No money. Just my dog-tags. I pull them out. They read:

Stanley Reader

Non-denomination

Born: 1983

USMC

Bloodstained, I throw them onto the table for good. I turn to the young woman to ask if she could spare a couple bucks. She's gone but the scent of lavender remains. Strange, I think. Then the ol' man turns around.

Did you try the roll yet?

Not yet.

319

Again that toothless smile, that greasy tangled hair, those deep weathered cracks, the broken spectacle, the faded overalls with mismatched socks and I think to myself…What a beautiful man. I bite into the roll, soft and sweet. And this time, I'm not so surprised. For indeed it's the best roll ever in my life… that ineffable sweetness…again. And I just stop trying to figure out where I am.

For it doesn't matter. I'm desperate.

-Remy Kirkham

Made in the USA
Las Vegas, NV
25 August 2022

54030332R00187